The Year
of the
Three-Legged Deer

ETH CLIFFORD

illustrated by Richard Cuffari

The Year
of the
Three-Legged
Deer

Houghton Mifflin Company Boston 1972

For David,
who nurtured both
the book and the author
and
for Ruthanne,
who brightens our life

Author's Note

A USUAL DISCLAIMER on the part of an author is the assertion that his characters are not intended to portray real people, alive or dead, but are purely fictional, created whole cloth from the author's imagination. The characters depicted in this manuscript are fictional, too, in that they came to life in the mind of this writer, but they were intended to be as much flesh and blood as any of the pioneers who gave of themselves to create a new world in the wilderness.

While none of these characters actually existed, some of the situations in which they find themselves did occur historically. Free Negroes, for example, were kidnaped at times; the silver disk and chain which Sakkaape receives in the book played a prominent part in the life of one freed slave, although the incident has been adapted loosely in order to fit it more properly into the framework of this particular narrative. White men did massacre an innocent Indian hunting party and became the first white men in Indiana to be tried, convicted and hung for injury to the red men.

Wherever possible, the book has been faithful to historical occurrences and scenes. However, in the interest of the narrative, it has been necessary to telescope time. This work, therefore, while attempting to be as accurate as possible, is not intended as an historical account.

Although the setting of the scenes, the description of the trading post, and the large house depicted in the opening chapter do exist and are authentic, it was in no way the intention of the author to render a biography of the early residents. For visitors to Indiana who might be interested in seeing the post and house, a trip to the Conner Prairie Pioneer Settlement and Museum in Noblesville, Indiana, would be most worthwhile. The buildings in the settlement include some of the original structures as well as restorations; the pioneer cabin in which Jesse might have lived with his Indian wife and children can be seen, as well as a trading post typical of the era, the loom house, the spring house, and, of course, the original William Conner Home, built in 1823.

I wish to thank Carl Smith, Associate Professor of Education at Indiana University, Bloomington, Indiana, for relating the charming incident of his encounter with a three-legged deer in Brown County and its remarkable adventures — its near brush with death when attacked by a savage wolf in its pen and again when, during a storm, it was washed down an arroyo. At first I contemplated the idea of a small book for children concerning the deer but having been intrigued for some time by the possibilities of utilizing the Conner Prairie Farm Settlement as background for a story and of applying some aspects of the Conner story to a fictional treatment, I was persuaded by my husband, David Rosenberg, whose critical judgment is highly appreciated and valued, to make an amalgam of both story ideas, placing the deer in a time slot that somehow seemed far more appropriate. My grateful thanks go, too, to Hubert Hawkins, Secretary of the Indiana Historical Society and head of the Indiana Historical Bureau, for his invaluable help in supplying source materials and for reading the manuscript to guard against glaring historical inaccuracies or inconsistencies.

Finally, I wish to thank my husband for giving me the typewriter, the time, and the encouragement it takes to tell a story.

ETH CLIFFORD
April 7, 1970
Indianapolis, Indiana

The Year
of the
Three-Legged Deer

Prologue

THE TALL YOUNG INDIAN studied the log cabin before him, but he did not enter. Instead he turned and followed a barely discernible path which dipped away from the hill on which the cabin stood. His eyes flicked across the field of tall, green, tasseled stalks and he paused for an instant, remembering this field in other days. For a moment he could almost see his people moving among the September corn, harvesting it for Jesse Benton, the man who was both farmer and trader, whose cabin he could still see from the slope in the hill.

Idly, the Indian continued to follow the path, which now moved down toward the river and then veered away to climb upward again past a shed shaded by huge elms. The young man turned his head and listened to the sound of a brook which trickled down the hill, disappeared into the recesses of the shed, and then emerged from the other side to continue its journey downward. The shed was a spring house, where perishable food was being kept chilled by the cool flowing water of the brook as it pursued its channeled course through troughs inside the shed. The young man went in and leaned down, letting the water flow across his finger tips. Straightening, he came out into the sun again where his wandering gaze came to rest at last on the imposing two-story brick house at the crest of the hill where it stood serenely facing the upper bank of the White River.

He stood and stared at the house a long time. At length he moved again, pausing in his climb to examine another building which stood a little way from the impressive home. He peered in through the open doorway to see a young woman absorbed in her work at a large loom, her plump cheeks lending a smiling appearance to her face although a frown of deep concentration creased her forehead. The Indian made no sound and the young woman's hands moved busily without pause at the loom. But when the Indian, having satisfied his curiosity, moved on, the young woman turned her head sharply, and then, with an obvious and urgent sense of uneasiness, rose suddenly to go and stare out the open doorway. The Indian was no longer in sight on the path, for by this time he had moved around the large brick house, gone past the well in the yard with only a passing glance to acknowledge its existence, and leaped lightly onto the spanking clean gray painted boards of the large open porch. He stared at the windows, then went closer to touch the panes, bright and sparkling in the daylight. Stepping back, he then turned his attention to some rockers aligned precisely along the porch. These, too, he touched, setting them gently swaying in the summer breeze which kept the rockers moving long after the Indian went into the house, as if it were a game between the two.

As the Indian entered the spacious hall, with its pale blue walls and its white wood paneling, a small girl came down the stairway that led to the foyer. Hearing footsteps, she paused and peered down between the square white slats of the banister, sitting down to get a better look at the intruder. She watched calmly as he entered the parlor, cocking her head to one side to listen intently to the sounds he made as he moved about the room where he was examining everything with childlike curiosity — the desk, the feathered pen in the inkwell, the gold-framed mirror above the pristine white fireplace wherein he examined himself impassively, then the two portraits that hung on either side of the room. She held her peace as he left the parlor and moved silently across the hall into the dining room. Here again he went from object to object, stopping at last to stare at a huge lazy Susan on the circular wood dining table. Outside the room, the little girl pressed her lips together and shook her head knowingly when she heard the lazy Susan spinning. The moment he reappeared she shrilled at him, "You're not supposed to play with the lazy Susan. Mama gets very mad when you play with it."

The Indian halted and stared up at her. She was standing now, arms akimbo, her deep blue eyes flashing with indignation, like a young puppy suddenly aware of its territorial prerogatives.

The Indian looked at her gravely.

"Where is the trader, little sister?" he asked.

The girl moved down another step.

"Are you a real Indian?" she asked, her anger gone like a sudden summer squall. "We don't have any more Indians around here, you know. Papa knew a lot of Indians. He grew up with them and lived in an Indian village and everything. That was before he married Mama and I was born. My name is Marybeth Benton. What's your name?"

"John," the Indian replied briefly.

"That's not an Indian name," the child cried.

"Anybody can have a name like John. Don't you have a real name?"

A smile hovered and disappeared as the Indian regarded the little girl. "They call me Takawsu. In the language of my people it means 'he is gentle.'"

"I wish I had an Indian name," the child said wistfully. She leaned over the banister. "If I was an Indian, what would my name be?"

The tall young man considered her. "I think," he said finally, his eyes glinting with amusement, "that your name would be Miin — that means 'small fruit,'" he added hastily, forestalling the next question that trembled on her lips. "Now tell me, little sister, do you know where the trader is?"

"Papa isn't a trader anymore. He's a senator," she said importantly. "He goes all the way to Indianapolis . . ." The Indian stared at her blankly. "Don't you know about Indianapolis?" she demanded incredulously. "Why it's the state capital. Papa helped plan it way back in eighteen twenty-one. Do you like Washington Street?" she prattled on, forgetting that he knew nothing about the city. "I do. Mama takes us in the carriage sometimes when she goes to the hatter's and Papa goes to Fancy Tom's — he's the barber, you know, and all the senators go to him because he was at Corydon with them when that was the capital, but I like the post office best, even though Mama lets me try on the hats. At the hatter's, I mean. So do Jonas and Jeremiah — like the post office, I mean. They're the twins, you know. They're boys but they're really very nice sometimes. Oh, you should see that post office when the mail stage comes in and you can hear the driver blowing on the horn he has and everybody comes running. You can hear that horn for *miles*, Mama says . . ."

The little girl broke off in the middle of her whirlwind monologue to stare fixedly behind the Indian. The young woman of the loom stood there, aiming a rifle with trembling fingers.

"Run, Marybeth," the young woman shrieked, when the Indian turned to see what sight had so effectively silenced his garrulous informant. She took a firmer grip on the rifle. "You murdering savage," she said grimly, "coming here to attack innocent children and women. Run, Marybeth."

"Oh, Susan!" Marybeth replied in exasperation. "This is Takawsu. That means 'he is gentle.' Put the rifle down," she coaxed. "There's a dear girl."

A smile warmed the Indian's face at the little girl's tone of voice. She was parroting someone expertly, probably her mother.

"Susan is our hired girl from the East," Marybeth explained rapidly. "She's afraid of everything."

"I am not," Susan objected hotly.

At this moment, two small boys exploded into the room, followed almost immediately by a tiny woman, who gave the impression of bustling even when standing still, and a tall rugged-looking man, with heavy brows knotted into a deep frown over eyes so darkly blue they appeared almost black. Startled by the boys, Susan tightened her finger and pulled back; a roar of gunfire filled the room and a picture tilted at a crazy angle on the far wall of the hall. Simultaneously both the girl and the woman screamed; Marybeth raced down the steps and hurled herself at the man, and the boys began whooping and dancing.

In the midst of the turmoil, Susan dropped the weapon to the floor and clapped her hands to her face.

"The baby!" she gasped.

"The baby?" The woman's face paled; her brown eyes seemed to grow enormous in her tiny face. "The baby! Something terrible has happened to the baby!"

"Nothing's *happened* to him," Susan assured her. "I just forgot that he's in the oven."

The woman's hand flew to her chest. "The *oven?*" she whispered. "You put Daniel in the *oven?*"

"There's no fire in the oven," Susan said,

aggrieved. "It just seemed a safe place to hide him at the time." She glared at the Indian.

The woman fled from the hall through a door into the kitchen, where she tore open the iron sheet across a brick oven high in the kitchen wall. Inside a baby lay curled, serenely napping. The mother snatched the infant from its cozy hideaway, whereupon the boy awoke and began to emit a lusty squalling at this sudden intrusion into his peaceful dozing.

In the hall, Mr. Benton stared at the young Indian above the head of the small girl, who was now held aloft in her father's arms.

"You have come," Mr. Benton said at last.

"I have come," the young man acknowledged.

"I have longed to see my first-born son. You are welcome," Jesse Benton said, his eyes studying the other, trying to assess the difference fifteen years had made. "How does Mekinges fare?"

"Mekinges my mother is dead," the young man replied somberly.

"And Sakkaape?"

"Dead, too. It has been a long time," Takawsu said briefly.

The children had fallen silent, turning their heads first to one man and then the other. In the kitchen, the baby's loud protests had finally dwindled away. Mrs. Benton returned to the hall.

"Jesse?" she asked questioningly.

"Forgive me, my dear," he replied. "This is Ta-kawsu — John, son of Mekinges."

"John Benton," the woman said clearly. "You are welcome here. Will you not come and have something to eat? I promise Susan will not shoot you," she added, enveloping him in the warmth of her smile.

Jesse Benton put Marybeth down. He beckoned to Takawsu. "While the women prepare some food," he said, "come and see the cabin where we lived, you and your mother and Chilili." Benton's voice faltered a moment.

"Chilili! What a pretty name," Marybeth said. "Who is Chilili?"

"A pretty one. Like you." Takawsu looked down at the little girl and smiled briefly.

The boys and Marybeth followed the two men out of the house, where all three promptly ran off to play a game. The men began to cross the field which dipped between the large house and the small rough cabin. Takawsu turned for a moment to stare back at the building they had just left, and then indicated the cabin with his head.

"The cabin we lived in is of no use to you now. Why does it still stand?"

9

"It was part of my life," Jesse Benton answered quietly. "A good part. A man likes to remember."

"I remember, too." Takawsu stared unseeingly at the land before him. "Many things. The trading post. Sakkaape. Chilili. That last year before we left this land . . ."

"The year of the three-legged deer," Jesse said, smiling.

"Yes." Takawsu stepped across the threshold of the cabin, which the two men had now reached. "Yes," he said again. "I too think of it always as the year of the three-legged deer." He looked about, his mind turning back fifteen years from this year of 1835 to the year 1819 when he had been a boy in this place.

1

OCTOBER – 1819

The Year Begins

Takawsu, the boy, waited impatiently for his father, Jesse Benton, and Pride Finch to get ready. Darkness enveloped the land early these cool fall nights. In the woods beyond the cabin, hunters were already stalking deer. John Duane, a visitor to the Benton cabin, had tired early of the talk and gone ahead, whistling his two dogs away from the fireplace where they had stretched out somnolently beside Takawsu. With him had gone Duane's indentured servant, a tall black man with somber eyes and a resolutely impassive expression. Duane ran a trading post thirty miles north of Jesse's post. He came at stated intervals to pick up the furs Jesse obtained from the trappers and the Delaware Indi-

11

ans, whose village was just across the White River, but he had never brought the "servant" Sam before, knowing Jesse Benton's feelings about this form of slavery. Throughout the evening, Takawsu, who had never visited Duane's trading post, eyed the Negro Sam surreptitiously, for this was the first time he had ever seen this *sakkaape*, this black man.

Duane had invited Takawsu to join him, but the boy had refused, preferring to wait and go with Jesse. The drone of the conversation made his eyes droop with weariness, for he found the talk of no particular interest. Pride Finch, a blacksmith by trade, had drifted in from some eastern settlement and was planning now to build a smithy nearby. There were horses to shoe, and hoes and other necessary implements to make for the few settlers already in the area and those who would most certainly be following. Settlers and Indians alike would need knives. Not a man anywhere, Pride Finch declared with quiet dignity, could make a better knife than Pride Finch. Most of all, however, Finch confessed, he had a pure hankering to make bells. Jesse glanced obliquely at Finch's hands. It seemed an unlikely task for those broad stubby fingers.

Was it true, Finch went on — he had heard some of the settlers talking — that bells were used in deer hunting? He himself was not a hunter, got what he needed in trade; but even an ignorant man like himself knew game had to be stalked with stealth . . .

Jesse laughed.

"It's a trick, you see," he said to Finch.

A bell was hung around a pony's neck, and the bowl of the bell stuffed with dry grass to keep the bell from tinkling until the time was right. Now Takawsu's attention was caught, but he remained silent. While Jesse explained, Takawsu thought of his own pony, as eager to take to the woods as Takawsu himself. Only last week Takawsu had taken his rifle and hunting knife, mounted his pony, and swung along the path behind the cabin into the depths of the forest.

Deer were plentiful, for it was still pōōkseet kēēshooh, the month of the broken moon, the month of the shedding of the leaves. The animals usually traveled in droves. Creatures of habit, they returned time and again to their favorite feeding places, following the trails and paths worn into the earth by their hoofs.

Takawsu stared into the crackling fire, a half smile touching his eyes. He had sighted the buck browsing near the edge of the stream that flowed just beyond the open glade in the woods. The buck, partly shaded from the early October morning sun by a weeping willow whose branches dipped almost to the surface of the shimmering water, had been nibbling tranquilly at the succulent water plants growing on the bank. Silently, Takawsu had dismounted. Then, working swiftly, Takawsu had freed the bowl of the bell, letting the dried grass twirl to the ground like a sprinkling of fine mist. He patted the pony and moved off to secure a hiding place behind some underbrush, careful to stay downwind from the grazing deer.

As soon as the bell was clear of the grass, the pony began to shake its head, and the sound of the bell rang like a clarion summons through the stillness of the crisp autumn air. The buck had lifted its great head and stared, its long ears standing alert, its antlers soaring majestically upward. The animal had not been frightened, only wide-eyed and curious. It had stood immobile, listening to the bell as it continued to peal, for the pony, well trained for the hunt, continued to shake its head. Unaware of the danger lurking in one young Indian boy's hands, the buck stood as in a trance. Takawsu took careful aim and fired, and the great deer fell crashing to the ground.

Takawsu brought his thoughts back to the present, for Jesse was now standing and stretching. At

14

length Jesse moved across the cabin, made an almost imperceptible gesture with his head to indicate to Takawsu that he was ready at long last, and lifted his rifle from the wooden pegs which held the weapon securely within his reach over the door.

"Ever go on a fire hunt before?" Jesse inquired of his guest.

Pride Finch shook his massive head. "Truth of the matter is," he confessed good-humoredly, wiping his broad nose vigorously with the back of a large, deeply veined hand, "I know a forge, and I know iron, and not much else."

"It's nothing like the bell on the pony, but I think we can promise you a night you won't forget," Jesse predicted.

Rifle in hand, Jesse stepped from the cabin into the moonlit night, followed by Finch and the boy, and moved down the hill which sloped toward the river and the canoe which Jesse and Takawsu had made together. They had felled a tree, from which they had cut and hollowed a log, leaving both the bow and stern solid. Then Jesse had bored a large hole in the bow, into which Takawsu had carefully jammed upright a strong solid piece of wood. On the upright Jesse had attached an iron frame, and from the frame suspended a torch.

When both men and Takawsu were in the canoe, Jesse lit the torch. The flame silhouetted

15

Pride Finch's huge bulk and sent ripples of light bouncing along the barrel of Jesse's rifle.

Normally Takawsu would have paddled, but Finch anticipated him. In his huge hands, the paddle seemed frail. At a sign from Jesse, Finch dipped the paddle into the water and sent the craft moving swiftly upriver. Before long, Takawsu's sharp ears caught the strident baying of dogs on the scent in the woods. In a moment, Finch also became aware of the dogs in the distance.

"Well," he said philosophically to his host, "it was a mighty short hunt. But then I never did expect to track any deer at night. Those fool dogs," he added, shaking his head. "Those Duane's, do you imagine?"

Jesse grinned. "I expect so. But the hunt isn't over. You might say it's hardly started."

"But those dogs . . ."

"Best old deer hunters you ever saw," Jesse reassured Finch. "They're chasing the deer to us right now."

Finch stared at Benton with suspicious eyes. Then a slow grin spread across his homely face. "I see how you do it," he said finally. "You just scare those animals to death with fire and noise."

"That's about the size of it," Jesse replied good-naturedly. "I don't rightly know the why or how of

16

it," he went on, "because most animals are afraid of fire. But the deer are different. To get away from the dogs, deer will just naturally make for the river. And when they see this fire going, they'll head straight on into it. They always head for the light. Plain curious, I expect."

Now Takawsu could hear the sound of crashing in the brush. He gestured sharply with his hand. In a low voice, Jesse told Finch to let the canoe drift with the current, but to hold his paddle steady so that the light of the torch faced the shore. Finch nodded to show that he understood.

Now a watchful stillness settled over the occupants of the canoe. A frog, quite near, kept up a commanding cry — *nee-deep, nee-deep*; a sudden breeze whipped some leaves across the bank in a swirl of whispering movements; the water made small lapping sounds against the sides of the canoe. Finch felt a mounting excitement; he flexed and unflexed his fingers rapidly against the paddle. Suddenly a doe, terrified and breathing hard, broke through the woods, saw the light, and paused, her flanks heaving. Then, as the dogs kept up their persistent shrilling, the doe seemed to aim herself directly at the path of light thrown across the water by the flaming torch. In his exhilaration, Finch forgot to remain silent and cried out, "She's heading right for us!" Simultaneously, Jesse's rifle spat death. The doe leaped in the air and then slumped to the ground.

Finch drew a deep breath, then released it with a shuddering sigh. "I just got plumb carried away," he apologized.

Jesse nodded. "No harm done." He turned to Takawsu. "We'll put you ashore. You can take care of the doe. I want to move on upriver a way."

"Want me to help him?" Finch asked. "Looks like kind of a lot of animal for the boy to handle on his own."

Jesse grinned. "Takawsu won't be carrying the doe home, though I expect he could with no trouble at all. He's just going to string her up on a sapling for now. We'll come back and tend to the skinning later."

Takawsu watched the canoe go skimming away from the bank. As it moved off, the glow of the torch receded, leaving only the familiar darkness and the faint shimmering of moonlight on the path. The woods were filled with night sounds: crickets near the bank of the river kept up a strident cacophony of communication; the call of the frogs grew more insistent; overhead a squirrel, disturbed by the gunfire, fled precipitously along the branch of a tree to another, in his passage dislodging the leaves in a miniature rustling shower.

18

These Takawsu noted and dismissed; they consti-
tuted no threat. What his sharp awareness did not
take note of, however, was the movement of a
shadowy figure skulking through the brush behind
him.

Takawsu reached the doe and, kneeling, ran his
hand over her flanks. There would be much good
meat to eat, and from the hide, leggings and moc-
casins, which Takawsu's young sister Chilili would
decorate. Intent upon the deer, Takawsu was
heedless of danger. When his senses finally alerted
him, it was too late. He saw a shadow pass across
the deer and tried to turn, but his hands were
seized roughly, pinioned behind him, and his face
pushed into the ground before he could cry out.

"Dog!" a voice whispered venomously in his ear.
"Son of a white man. Tonight you die. The white
man will die." A knife appeared in the intruder's
hand; it flicked out and back; a slash in Takawsu's
ear dripped red. Takawsu's wrists and then his an-
kles were lashed together, and then Takawsu was
lifted and dropped roughly against a tree, where he
sat helplessly, but able to see his attacker clearly at
last. The man before him was tall and muscular; in
his face, which bore angry gashes of color, his large
black eyes were luminous with hate; his hair, pulled
back in a tight knot behind his head, glinted blue-
black in the moonlight.

19

"Behold your enemy," the man rasped. "Stone Eater, son of Winnamac, friend to Tecumseh, the Shooting Star, destroyer of the long knives."

Takawsu stared. "But Tecumseh is dead," he whispered, surprised. "He has been dead a long time. The war with the white man is long over as well."

Stone Eater struck his chest with a clenched fist in a sharp gesture. "Shooting Star is dead, but Stone Eater lives. The war lives" — once again Stone Eater struck his chest defiantly — "here. Shooting Star said the white man is like a fat dog that carries its tail on its back but when frightened drops it between his legs and runs away. Son of a white dog! Is your tail between your legs?"

"I am the son of Mekinges, daughter of a chief," Takawsu replied angrily. "I am from the Lenni Lenape, 'men who are men.' You will not see my tail between my legs."

"'Men who are men,'" the other mocked. "The Lenni Lenape are women. Women and children."

"Brave warrior," Takawsu said contemptuously, ignoring the danger of baiting the man who held him prisoner, "have you come to do battle with women and children?"

Stone Eater brought his painted face close to Takawsu's. "I destroy all my enemies. You shall die and the white man who bred you shall die. He will watch his flesh die and we will see if he too is a woman who will cry in fear."

He bound Takawsu's mouth, so the boy could make no warning sound. As he bent to his task, a shadow moved behind him and blended with other shadows. Takawsu's sharp eyes caught the movement and his heart leaped within him. Had one of the hunters returned and seen the ambush? Once again the shadow shifted, and this time Takawsu caught a brief glimpse of the man who moved so silently. It was the *sakkaape* — the black man. Takawsu's hopes dimmed. The *sakkaape* had no weapons. Even should he attempt to rescue Takawsu — and of this Takawsu had little expectation — the black man would be helpless against the armed and ruthless Stone Eater.

The *sakkaape* stood a moment, appraising the situation, then searched noiselessly for a large stone. Finding one that satisfied him, he flung it into the brush behind Stone Eater. The Indian whirled away from the boy; simultaneously the black man emerged from the shadows and hurled himself at the Indian. The men battled in grim silence until Stone Eater, flinging himself violently away from the Negro, was able to draw his tomahawk and knife from his belt.

"So the slave is so well trained he fights like a

dog for his master?" Stone Eater taunted his opponent.

The black man did not answer, but kept his eyes warily on the Indian who now began to circle him, tomahawk clenched in his left hand, knife in his right. Suddenly Stone Eater's right hand shot forward; the *sakkaape* leaped back, but not before the point of the knife drew blood from his arm. Again the Indian circled; again the knife moved in Stone Eater's hand like the darting strike of a rattler; again he drew blood.

In the fight, the men had drawn closer to Takawsu. The boy, his eyes never leaving the combatants, inched slowly away from the tree. The black man, facing the boy, took note. He turned and retreated from Stone Eater's charge, bringing him closer to where the boy waited. Stone Eater lunged; the black man leaped nimbly aside, and Takawsu hurled himself flat on the ground, his legs thrust forward. Stone Eater tripped and fell, the tomahawk spinning from his grasp, but he clutched the knife in a firm grip even as he hit the ground. In a flash, the black man was astride him; the knife glinted in the moonlight as both men struggled desperately for possession of the weapon. In a final spurt of strength, the black man, who was now panting heavily from the exertion of battle, wrested the knife from Stone Eater's hand.

"Kill him! Kill him!" Takawsu's eyes commanded. Stone Eater waited stoically for the knife to plunge into his heart. That it would he did not doubt for an instant. But the black man rose, releasing Stone Eater from his weight. Instantly the Indian sprang to his feet.

"You show mercy?" he spat. "Mercy is for women. We will meet again, you and I." He cast a last venomous glance at Takawsu and melted into the sheltering darkness of the forest.

The black man kneeled beside Takawsu and began to cut through the leather strips that held him fast. When Takawsu was free, he said bitterly, meanwhile massaging the blood back into his wrists, "You should have killed him. He would have killed me. And you. And my father. He has sworn to kill us all."

For the first time, the black man spoke. "I am a slave," he said coldly, "but I am not a savage."

He turned away from the boy as John Duane's dogs came bounding along the path, Duane, Finch, and Jesse behind them, carrying the deer they had successfully hunted down. Duane, seeing the knife still in the Negro's hands, snapped suspiciously, "What's going on here, Sam? What are you doing with that knife?"

Before the black man could speak, Takawsu rushed to his defense. With the words falling rapidly from his lips, he told the men everything that had occurred, repeating Stone Eater's final threats. During the recital, the black man stood aside silently, neither adding to nor corroborating Takawsu's tale. When at last Takawsu, too, fell silent, Jesse stepped forward.

"I'd like to shake your hand," he said simply.

Duane stepped deliberately into Jesse's path. "There's no call to do that," he said in a low voice. "He'll only get uppity. You've got to keep them in their place. You know how these niggers are."

Jesse stared at Duane, and just as deliberately moved around him. "I don't see a nigger," he said in a clear voice. "I see a man. I see a very brave man."

For the balance of the evening, Jesse seemed lost in his thoughts. Every once in a while, as the men skinned and dressed the deer they had killed, he cast thoughtful glances at the black man. Then, having almost visibly come to a decision, he called John Duane aside.

"John," he asked, "did you mean what you said, earlier this evening, about being tired of running the post and wanting to go further west for a while?"

"Every word," Duane assured him. "You know what it's been lately. The beaver catch isn't near what it used to be." He chewed reflectively on a long piece of grass. "And now that the government's bought the land from the Indians, this area is going to be swarming with settlers." He shook his head. "It's getting a mite too civilized for my taste. Tell you the truth, Jesse, I'm not a man to put down roots. I've been here too long as it is. Sure would like to take off with Jim Peters when he heads west . . . knows the country out there like the back of his hand, he tells me . . ."

"I'll be glad to take the post off your hands," Jesse offered, and added offhandedly "and Sam, too. I'll buy his contract," he said hastily, as Duane gave him a quizzical look.

"Fixing to set him free?" Duane asked. "Don't tell me different, Jesse. I've seen that look in your eye before."

"Can't see how it would make much difference to you," Jesse said persuasively. "If I take the post off your hands, I'll need someone to run it. And I know for a fact Sam's been in charge there while you've been off trapping . . ."

Duane laughed. He took Jesse's arm and the two men moved off, talking earnestly. Finally they shook hands. When the men returned, Jesse approached the black man as if by chance.

"Listen, Sam," he began diffidently, rubbing his long fingers over the creases in his forehead, "John Duane and I — we've been doing a little palavering

26

just now, and the upshot of it is, I've bought your contract."

The black man faced him impassively. He had been bought and sold before.

"Well, like I say," Jesse went on, "I've got the contract now. And as soon as I can get the papers, you're a free man." The black man stood motionless, his face frozen. "I'll go up to Corydon first thing in the morning and have the papers made out." Jesse turned away, then came back, as if with an afterthought. "By the way, Sam, I bought the trading post from Duane, too. I'd consider it a mighty big favor if you'd take it on for me. I sure would hate to have to start out with a new man."

"You mean the *sakkaape* is a free man, just like that?" Takawsu, who had overheard the conversation, asked with surprise.

"Just like that," Jesse replied, then added sharply, "And he has a name. There's no need to keep calling him the black man."

"No," the Negro said. "I had no name. I had a handle, a convenience. From now on, I should like to be called Sakkaape. It says truly what I am." He extended his hand. "I thank you."

Jesse Benton stared at his son, and then back at Sakkaape. He gripped the other man's hand firmly. "Friends don't need to be thanked or to thank."

Finch, who had approached the little group and

27

had overheard the last words spoken, yawned and said sleepily, "Listen, friends, can we get back to the cabin? I've got an early start ahead of me to-morrow."

"Sure," Jesse reassured him. "I've got to make an early start tomorrow too."

2

WINTER HAD WITHDRAWN from the land, bidding it good-night. In the camp of the Lenni Lenape, it was time for the ritual ceremony of the first hunt of the new season. The sachem arranged the hunt carefully; to each of his people, he gave the command to take up an assigned position in a circle within the radius of a mile. Each man rooted up the grass in the position assigned to him and then carefully set fire to it. The fire lapped greedily at the dry grass, leaping from the outer rim of the human circle inward. Behind the fire came the hunters in full cry, filling the early spring air with a horrisonant caterwauling before which the animals trapped within the circle fled in terror. The circle tightened; rifles exploded; soon the Lenni Lenape would eat their fill. After the feast would come the burnt offerings, the songs, and the dances.

It did not seem possible for a single animal to escape the ring of death, yet a bear cub, weighing about one hundred pounds and smarting from a slight wound in its shoulder where a bullet had grazed it, slipped from the circle during the organized frenzy unseen by all except Takawsu.

Rifle in hand, hunting knife secure in his belt, Takawsu followed the cub into the forest. Behind him came the sound of the singing: *hagginj, ha, ha, ha; hagginj ha; hagginj ha, hagginj ha, ha, ha, ha.* Ahead of Takawsu, the cub crashed through a thicket, crying for its mother. Takawsu shook his head when he heard the whimpering complaint, remembering a time when he had gone hunting with his uncle, Winikiso, who was named for the snow month. Winikiso had shot and wounded a huge black bear; the animal had fallen to the ground and immediately set up a series of sad complaints, like a panther gnawed by unendurable hunger pangs. Winikiso had regarded the bear with vexation.

"Will you not finish him off?" Takawsu had asked, surprised that his uncle stood watching the bear with a contemplative eye.

Winikiso had not answered, but had moved closer to the bear. Suddenly he had made an angry gesture with his right hand clenched. "You are a coward, bear!" He spat the words at the wounded animal at his feet. "And I thought you were a warrior! Does a warrior cry and whimper like an old woman! I tell you the truth when I say your tribe has conquered my tribe from time to time. If you had conquered me, I would have borne it with courage. I would have died like a warrior. But you! You sit and cry. Coward! You disgrace your tribe."

Winikiso stepped back. His rifle roared, and the piteous wailing stopped.

"Uncle," said the amazed Takawsu, "do you think he understood your words?"

"He understood," Winikiso said positively. "He knew the fortune of war. He knew that one or the other of us must have fallen. Yet he died like an old woman. Not so with Winikiso. Winikiso would not have disgraced his nation."

Winikiso had died in the summer of Takawsu's sixth year, in the month of the time of raising the earth about the corn, from a disease with the curious name of smallpox. When Winikiso was buried, the chief had talked earnestly to Winikiso, beseeching him to forget those whom he had left behind. For three days after Winikiso was in his grave, Takawsu had visited it with the other relatives, helping to build the little fire which was then

31

immediately put out after the first blaze; the fire had liberated Winikiso's spirit.

Takawsu did not think often of Winikiso anymore, but the wounded bear cub had brought him back to mind vividly. "I will scold the little bear," Takawsu reflected as he continued to track the cub, following its trail deeper into the forest. Suddenly the cries of the cub died away, to be replaced by a new sound, as if a number of wild animals were locked in deadly combat.

Takawsu approached the arena of sound warily and then paused, unable at first to credit the scene before him. Two huge black bears stood erect, like pugilists in a ring taking careful measure of each other, growling in rage at two snarling panthers who were bedeviling them. A doe lay on the ground, torn and bleeding, a victim of a panther attack and now the source of contention between the bears and the original hunters. Takawsu's glance briefly flicked from the doe to the glade beyond the fray. He wondered if this were the same doe he and Chilili had seen five short days ago, in this very glen.

Chilili went to the creek to pluck shoots and Takawsu accompanied her through the forest, for he was going fishing. Although Chilili was only eleven, and Takawsu fourteen, it would never have occurred to Takawsu to help his sister. Plucking shoots, curing hides, working in the garden — these were women's pursuits. Nor did the girl expect her brother to share her tasks.

They came upon the doe unexpectedly, at a time when she was about to birth a fawn. Driven instinctively by the need to protect and shelter her unborn young, the doe had sought out this secluded place in the woods. Their curiosity aroused, Takawsu and Chilili found a hiding place from which they watched the doe with grave interest. Beyond the open glade, already green with the promise of good grazing, they could glimpse the creek glinting where the rays of the early morning spring sun touched the water, and farther on, rippling dark and brooding to mingle with the shadows.

The doe, having reached the glen, stopped and raised her head high, sniffing the breeze, searching the land. She had never given birth before, but all her senses were alert to the dangers that threatened the new life within her. Bears haunted the area; panthers dropped murderously from branches of trees on unsuspecting game. She herself had never been attacked, but she had witnessed many a kill — the giant leap of the panther, the flash of razor-sharp claws, the smell of blood and death — these were seared into her memory. And instinct warned her that the new life within her was particularly vulnerable to attack.

The birth pangs began. She could wait no longer. Quickly the doe had trampled down the grass in the glen. Now nothing mattered but the arrival of the new fawn.

Takawsu turned to smile at his sister. The girl was watching the doe intently, her deep blue eyes so like Jesse's serious, her delicately shaped face held angled but motionless lest she disturb the gentle creature now in labor. Chilili was like a miniature replica of Jesse; Takawsu, with his sturdy frame and large bones, was instantly recognizable as the son of Mekinges. Chilili did not turn, but her hand shot out to grasp Takawsu's arm — a limp, tiny wet creature had just emerged from the doe's body to lie supinely on the ground beside its mother. At once the doe began the arduous task of cleaning her fawn. With rapid movements of her tongue, she licked the infant creature's fur; again and again she nudged and pushed the fawn into new positions, determined to get at every area of its body. Then, as instinctively as she had selected the glen, she cleared the mucus from the fawn's nose so that the newborn creature might begin to breathe more easily. Satisfied at last that her young was thoroughly clean, the doe resumed her nudging.

Patiently she persisted until the fawn rose and stood on its still wobbly feet.

Now Chilili turned at last to her brother, her face joyous, her eyes filled with laughter. She knew that this tiny brown creature, whose fur was spotted with white hair, would before long run swiftly at its mother's side, ready to leave this nursery so carefully prepared for it by the doe. But at this moment, it presented a comical appearance; the mere act of standing confronted it with an almost insurmountable problem. The fawn's legs would go sprawling and time and again it would fall helplessly to the ground.

The doe maintained her watchful care; each time the fawn fell, the doe nudged it back onto its feet. At last the fawn took its first weak shaky steps. Having done so, it immediately sought its reward. It pushed at its mother with determination and finally began to nurse, drinking in the rich warm milk greedily. Contented and full at last, the fawn curled itself up on the grass and went to sleep. It was only then that the doe rose to forage for food for herself so that she could go on nursing her hungry infant. She seemed to be unconcerned now for the fawn's safety. She had chosen the glen with great care; in the dappled sunlight filtering through the trees, the equally dappled infant, lying peacefully asleep, was almost invisible. Had Chilili and Takawsu not witnessed the birth, they might never even have suspected the presence of this new life in the forest. The fawn was too young to give off the musky odor that attracted its predators. As long as the infant did not move, it was fairly safe.

A scream from one of the panthers brought Takawsu's mind back to the present with a jolt. The shrieking panther had soared over one of the bears in an attempt to attack it from behind but the bear had swiveled to face the charge, dealing the panther a violent blow across its head. Somewhat dazed, the panther sought refuge in a nearby tree, where, from an overhanging branch, it spat and snarled at the bears below. The other panther continued to make quick rushing movements which the bears parried expertly with their huge arms.

Takawsu looked up, his spine tingling with the portent of danger. There above him, the panther stared down malevolently, body poised to spring. Takawsu fired rapidly and with a rasping cry, the panther fell to the ground, where it lay raging and helpless, tearing at the ground in fury. In the din of the fracas, the other animals either did not hear or elected to ignore both the shot and the wounded panther, for the struggle between them

continued unabated. The second panther pursued the tactics of the first; every little while it sprang over the bears, high above their heads. The smaller bear swung its left arm in a vicious arc as the panther made another wild leap. It missed, but the panther swerved and in doing so came within reach of the larger bear which dealt the panther so stinging a blow it was knocked almost senseless ten feet away. Recovering, the panther climbed about thirty feet up the tree closest to it and stretched its sinuous bulk across a large limb, where it lay regarding the bears with narrowed eyes. Once again the sound of Takawsu's rifle rang through the forest. The panther in the tree screamed, then leaped from the branch into a thick clump of brush and vanished into the woods.

Now at last the bears looked about, as if uncertain, aware at last of an intrusion in their battle. Finally, as if by some silent agreement, both bears dropped back on all fours and fled. The wounded panther which lay on the ground shrieked imprecations until Takawsu approached it and dispatched it with a single shot. Then he returned to the tree from which the second panther had leaped to the ground. Finding no trace of blood, he concluded that his shot had frightened but not wounded the animal.

Takawsu went to the doe and studied it. It lay

where it had fallen, raked and torn by the sharp claws of the panthers. Takawsu wondered if the battle he had witnessed between the bears and the panthers had been precipitated by the kill. At last Takawsu gave thought to the fawn. Had it survived, or had it, too, died, terrified and helpless, in the savage free-for-all? Takawsu approached the glen quietly; had he not known where to look he might have missed seeing the fawn completely, so still did it lie in the dappled light. He kneeled beside the small creature of the woods, and an unaccustomed surge of pity filled him. The fawn was alive, but only faintly so, for it had not escaped attack after all. One leg lay almost completely severed where it had been savagely mauled by one of the panthers. The doe must have leaped to the fawn's defense, but neither mother nor infant was equal to the cunning and swiftness of the predator.

Takawsu lifted his rifle again. The most sensible thing would be to relieve this suffering creature of what little life it still had. At that moment, the fawn opened its eyes and fixed Takawsu with a soft mournful look, a glance that reminded Takawsu of his gentle sister. So Chilili had looked when Jesse had brought home a wolf cub he had found in the forest four years before. The cub had been spared and was now Chilili's faithful companion.

On impulse Takawsu lifted the fawn and carefully draped it across his shoulders. Jesse would know what to do. And if the animal was meant to live, Chilili's love would nurture it. Takawsu turned from the glen, his body burdened but his spirit curiously light. There would be no more hunting this day. It was time to go home.

3

———

Takawsu stepped away from the trading post and stood quietly in the morning sun. His glance ranged over the fertile open prairie which sloped down for acres before it met the banks of the Wapahani, the White River. In the months to come this choice bottom land lying in the horseshoe bend of the river would be covered with corn, the spiked tassels of the plants rippling beneath the gentle breezes of summer. But now, at the end of May, Tauwinipen, the planting month, the rolling countryside gave no hint of seedlings ready to sprout.

Behind Takawsu, Chilili sat cross-legged on the ground, her head bent, her deep blue eyes narrowed, concentrating on her task. She was sewing ribbons on a blue broadcloth dress. Under her skillful fingers a handsome border had already begun to emerge, not so fine as Mekinges would wish perhaps but still undoubtedly decorative. Later Mekinges might help Chilili add silver brooches to the garment.

Takawsu turned his glance toward the cabin. Beyond the small log structure, where the land moved in a gentle slope down to a small stream, a little deer grazed contentedly within a fenced-in area. Not too far from the deer a large gray wolf, her fur tinged with a hint of black, sprawled indolently, her eyes riveted in an unblinking, watchful stare on the grazing animal. Smiling, Takawsu walked to the enclosure. The wolf stirred, lifting her great head, and studied Takawsu gravely. For the moment, she seemed tame and gentle as any dog, relaxed and lethargic in the warmth of the spring sun, but last night, her yellow eyes gleaming balefully in the moonlight, her chilling howls had quivered across the land and she had been all wolf, wild and terrifying.

"Do not fear, Ahtu," Takawsu reassured the wolf. "I will not harm the little one."

As Takawsu watched approvingly, the deer came bounding to the fence at the sound of his voice. It was still difficult for Takawsu to believe that the soft-eyed fawn, its red coat sleek and glossy in the sunlight, running so sure-footedly and carefree within the enclosure, as fleetly as any deer in the forest, had but three legs. When Takawsu reached across the fence and began to rub his hand gently along the fawn's face, the wolf rose and moved to Takawsu's side.

"See, Maskanako," Takawsu murmured to the deer. "See how Ahtu watches over you. Even I must be careful when I touch you." The fawn broke away suddenly, gamboled around the enclosure, and came back to stand quietly under Takawsu's gentle caress. "Was it not a good name for him, Ahtu?" Takawsu smiled down at the wolf. "Maskanako, 'he is strong.' "

Takawsu remembered well how the fawn came to be named. He had come from the forest, the fawn limp and dying over his shoulders, and burst into the cabin. Mekinges, stirring blue dye in a great kettle in the fireplace, her long black hair lying in a thick braid down her back, turned and stared at her son. Jesse Benton was arranging heavy white blankets on the shelves; along the edge of each blanket there was a series of blue stripes, some long and some short. A blanket having one short and two long stripes required the exchange of two large beaver pelts and one small — the Lenni Lenape knew Jesse marked everything fairly and

43

were content. Jesse too turned at the sound of Takawsu's quick entrance into the cabin.

"Clear the table," Takawsu commanded his sister, who had followed him into the cabin. She did as she was told quickly and without question, her eyes wide and troubled.

"Is it the little one we saw in the forest?" she asked softly, lest a louder tone disturb the creature spread limp and lost on the rough wooden surface. Takawsu nodded curtly. Mekinges and Jesse had drawn close to the table, and now were both staring somberly down at the animal.

"It is dying," Mekinges said. "Why do you bring it?"

"It is my sister's fawn," Takawsu appealed to his mother. "We saw it born. Mekinges my mother has the healing power in her hands. She will make the animal well."

Mekinges shook her head. "I have the healing power," she replied drily, "but I do not have the gift of life. The animal clings to life by a whisper."

"But it clings," Chilili pleaded.

Jesse laid a gentle hand on his daughter's head. "It is better dead," he said. Chilili's head moved restlessly under his hand, but Jesse held her. "Look at the animal," he commanded. "The leg is almost severed from the body. It would have to be amputated. Even if it survived, which I seriously doubt, how would it walk and run on three legs?"

Chilili ran her hand delicately along the side of the fawn's face. As she did so, the fawn opened its eyes briefly; they were clouded with pain and shock. Her own eyes misted with tears.

"Please," she whispered to Mekinges. Mekinges turned to look at her husband; he nodded, an almost imperceptible gesture, and she acquiesced.

"Go quickly," she commanded the children. "I will need certain herbs from the woods." Rapidly she named the roots and leaves they were to collect. Almost before Mekinges had finished speaking Chilili fled from the cabin, Takawsu just behind her.

Mekinges looked down at the deer. "It is a foolish thing to do," she said practically. "A three-legged deer!"

Jesse examined his hunting knife, then studied the mangled leg intently. "It should not even be alive." He shrugged. "But since it is, and it is Chilili's . . ." He shrugged his shoulders again and left the thought unfinished. Mekinges regarded her husband with smiling eyes; she knew only too well the special place Chilili occupied in his heart.

While Mekinges made a poultice from the roots and herbs Chilili and Takawsu brought, Jesse deftly removed the fawn's leg. Chilili turned away but Takawsu watched resolutely, ready to aid his father however he could. When the poultice was in place, Mekinges said, "It will live or it will die. We can do nothing more."

"It will live," Chilili insisted. "I will talk in its ear. It will know my voice."

Mekinges went back to the kettle of blue dye; Jesse returned to his task of filling the shelves which lined the north wall of the combination trading post and living quarters. "You must return to your tasks, my daughter," Mekinges called from the fireplace.

"I cannot leave." Chilili's tone was final. "If I leave, he will die."

"Then you must stay, little sister," Takawsu said gently.

Outside the day declined gradually; the sun died in a frenzy of color across the horizon; the sky darkened and surrendered to night. Chilili kept her post. She slept fitfully in a chair pulled close to the deer's head; from time to time as sleep tugged at her lids her body drooped and her head dipped, but she forced herself to wake and whisper soft soothing sounds into the animal's ear. In the morning, Jesse found Chilili, her arms around the fawn, her head resting on the table beside the head of the animal, both sleeping soundly. Jesse shook

Chilili gently. She woke with a start, her first concern for the fawn.

"It's all right," Jesse said, smiling. "It is sleeping."

"Sleeping? Not . . ." Her voice faltered.

"Sleeping. A good sign." Jesse moved across the cabin and out into the fresh morning air. He did this every morning he was home, his eyes sweeping the land. He had a deep, quiet, abiding love for this land. Every bush, every blade of grass, each rise and dip were as familiar to him as the sharp command of the cardinal issuing from the branch of the maple tree beside the cabin and the reticent "bobwhite" from the quail nesting in the woods.

Chilili joined him, her eyes shadowed and her small face pinched with fatigue. In a moment Takawsu also stepped from the cabin.

"Well, little sister," he greeted her, smiling. She smiled back. "I see the little animal lives."

"Maskanako lives," she agreed gravely.

"So? Maskanako?" Jesse's eyebrows shot up. "It has a name?"

"Maskanako," Chilili repeated. " 'He is strong.' I told him this in the night. He knows. It is a good name for him. He knows it."

"Have you thought how you will feed him . . . Maskanako?" asked Jesse.

"Grass . . . I will bring grass," Takawsu offered.

Jesse shook his head. "Not grass. Not yet. It is too young, too small. Maskanako needs a mother's milk."

Chilili bit her lip thoughtfully, her eyes worried.

"Ahtu has lost her litter," Takawsu suggested.

Jesse exploded into laughter. "A *wolf?* Nurse a deer?"

Chilili tugged urgently at Jesse's hand.

"Ahtu would do it for me," she said. Jesse looked down at his daughter's hopeful face. He honkered back on his heels so that their eyes were level. "Listen, my child," he began. "They are enemies. Natural enemies. Do you understand? Ahtu will destroy the little creature. She cannot help it. It is her nature."

Chilili stared into her father's eyes, so concerned, so like her own. "Ahtu will do it for me," she repeated. "When Maskanako wakes, we will carry him here. We will make a bed for him in the grass. And Ahtu will feed him."

All that day, Maskanako slept. When Mekinges changed the poultices, he stirred in his sleep but did not open his eyes. It was not until the next day, after Chilili had spent another restless night at his side, that the soft brown eyes focused on the deep blue eyes of the young girl. The deer tried to lift its head but Chilili pressed it back to the table. "Not yet, my brave Maskanako, not yet."

Later Jesse carried the fawn to a bed of grass lovingly prepared by Chilili with Takawsu's help and laid it down gently so that the wound would not come in contact with the ground. Ahtu, stretched full length some little space away, regarded the activity suspiciously. When the fawn caught the wolf's scent, it struggled in terror to rise and flee. Jesse kept it firmly in place but once again he cautioned Chilili, "Even if Ahtu will nurse it, the fawn will not drink the milk. It is too frightened. It smells its enemy."

"They will learn," Chilili insisted, pressing her lips together in a stubborn line. She summoned Ahtu. The wolf rose and circled warily, mouth drawn back in a preliminary snarl. "No," Chilili reprimanded sharply. She went to the wolf and dug her hands into the fur at the nape of its neck. Clutching the fur, she guided the wolf to where the deer lay trembling. "Lie down!" she commanded. The wolf stood rooted, eyes narrowed, its tongue lapping over its teeth. "Lie down!" Chilili said again, pushing the wolf hard. Ahtu turned and stared at Chilili. Once more Chilili issued the firm command, pointing to the ground as she did so. Jesse and Takawsu watched but said nothing. Chilili had taken over both animals — they would obey or not, as they willed it, and neither Jesse nor

Takawsu could change the order of things. At last Ahtu sank to the ground. Chilili, her face intent, motioned to her father and brother. "You must place Maskanako so he can feed. Quickly," she urged them.

"We hear you," Jesse replied gravely. Takawsu and Jesse did as Chilili asked, but instantly Ahtu snarled a warning, and Maskanako refused the nipple. Jesse shook his head. "You ask too much of them," he sighed. But Chilili would not yield. "Maskanako must have milk. He must drink or die. He will drink." Again and again Chilili tried to force the fawn to feed without success. Chilili looked at her father, tears spilling from her eyes.

"Wait," Jesse said. He leaned over Ahtu, tugging at the nipple until milk flowed on his finger. He forced his finger into the fawn's mouth. Once, twice, three times. The fourth time he edged the fawn's mouth up against the nipple. At last the fawn began to feed. Ahtu turned her great head and stared at the stranger drawing strength and life from her body. Jesse held his breath. If Ahtu rejected the fawn now, the little creature was doomed. Chilili put her hands together and clenched them against her chest. Ahtu stared at her and then dropped her head against the ground, her yellow eyes staring off into space. Maskanako nuzzled and drank. At last she finished feeding. Content, she curled up against Ahtu and promptly fell asleep. Ahtu did not move.

Chilili turned and gave her father a tremulous smile. "Ahtu will not harm Maskanako now. Maskanako is her child now. You will see."

"I have already seen, little miracle worker," Jesse replied with a grin.

The fawn had come to them in March; now, at the end of May, the deer was racing across the field in gay abandon.

Chilili joined her brother at the fence. "He is beautiful," Chilili said. "Even with three legs, he is beautiful."

Takawsu nodded. He left Chilili standing at the fence and went back to the front of the cabin. Soon Sakkaape would be arriving with supplies for the trading post. With Jesse gone to Corydon on business, it was Takawsu's job to put the supplies on the shelves and pack the furs on the mules for Sakkaape's return trip.

4

———

Takawsu yawned. He had risen early, for this morning he and Sakkaape were leaving Jesse's trading post to carry furs back to the post Sakkaape was running thirty miles to the north. Takawsu stood waiting impatiently, looking back at the cabin every few minutes, wondering how much longer Sakkaape would linger inside talking to Mekinges. When Sakkaape was ready, he and Takawsu would follow the trail which skirted the double log cabin and snaked its way through the dense forest of walnut, maple, and sycamore trees that rimmed the open plains that Jesse farmed. Takawsu knew the trail well, for a number of times since Sakkaape had taken over the post from John Duane, both he and Sakkaape had led pack horses, weighted with the

53

skins trappers brought to Jesse — beaver, of course, but also raccoon, muskrat, skunk, and even wildcat, wolf, and more rarely bear — to the other trading post. From there, the furs went further north and east, where men eagerly exchanged them for silver. Jesse had told Takawsu that beaver especially brought good prices. Across the sea, Jesse explained, in a country called France, men wore hats and coats trimmed with beaver. It was a sign of affluence, of importance. Jesse laughed and shrugged. The customs of other nations were strange but they were filling his trunk with silver dollars. Jesse kept the trunk at the head of his bed. Right now it was filled with over a bushel of silver. When Jesse was home, he slept with his rifle at easy reach, but strangely enough, the door to the cabin was never locked.

"Lock it?" Jesse had said in wonder one day when Sakkaape had questioned him. "Why? who would steal from me?" Not the settlers. And not the Delawares. He had lived among them all of his life. Never had he seen a bolt or a lock on a cabin. When, for whatever reason, a man left his home, he placed a log against the door. It was his sign which said, "I am not at home, but all that is within is mine." Jesse had grinned. "If you like, I'll put a log against the door whenever I go to Corydon."

Sakkaape had said then, quietly, "And when I am here, when you are gone?"

Jesse had given the other a long, reflective stare. "When you are here, and I am not," he had answered finally, "then there's no need for a log, is there?"

Sakkaape had grinned. "No need." He had fingered an ornament which hung from a silver chain around his neck as he spoke. Jesse had brought the silver chain and disk when he had returned from Corydon where he had filed the necessary papers that made Sakkaape a free man. It had been a purchase of impulse. In the courthouse, when he had filled out all the forms, including a full history of Sakkaape's brave defense of Takawsu, the clerk had laughed and muttered, "Too bad your nigger can't wave these here papers around, let folks know what he done."

"Well now, that's a right good idea," Jesse had drawled. "Glad you thought of it."

"Now hold on," the clerk had pulled the forms away, "you can't have these. They gotta stay here. They're court records." He had snickered. "Why doncha get him a collar and hang it 'round his neck?"

Jesse had had the silver disk specially made, and on it was engraved a brief description of Sakkaape's rescue of Takawsu, together with the announcement that Sakkaape was a free man. Sakkaape had worn the medallion proudly since the first moment Jesse had handed it to him.

That winter Sakkaape had come often to Jesse's trading post, for this was the season that furs were plentiful. Often when he arrived, he found Jesse and Takawsu pressing the furs into bales, using a primitive press worked by wedges. The pelts, having been sorted carefully, were then packed in bales and put on waiting horses. Sometimes Takawsu accompanied Sakkaape on the trip back. Even with the sure-footed animals, it was a difficult trail to cover, for it wandered almost imperceptibly through the dense woods, along the slippery banks of swollen creeks; beyond the gentle rises that threaded the land, it edged low-lying swamps, deadly and deceptive. Sudden rainfalls often mired the path until the mud was knee-deep; here and there rotting and dying trees created barriers that were unpassable. Then the horses had to be guided roundabout, tiring animals and humans alike as miles were added to the already distant post. Coming back was easier for Takawsu. Leaving the laden horses with Sakkaape at the trading camp, Takawsu was able to cover the ground swiftly, his rifle shoulder-borne, his knife sheathed at his side. Sometimes Takawsu also carried a tomahawk. Bears might challenge him in the woods and he had seen packs of wolves snarling after deer. Here, too, panthers prowled or perched in the forks of branches, their eyes narrow and observing, ready to strike at game.

What was keeping Sakkaape, Takawsu wondered, shifting his weight restlessly from one foot to the other. He turned to stare at the double log cabin, as if by staring he could will Sakkaape to come through the door. Suddenly Ahtu bounded to his side, her teeth bared, a low snarling sound vibrating the muscles in her throat. Takawsu turned from his contemplation of the cabin to see four white men approaching quietly, rifles in hand. The leader of the group was tall and slender and walked with his head thrust forward. His gray-blond hair, which nearly grazed his shoulders, was swept back from his high forehead. His faded blue eyes seemed almost colorless. A second, older man was quite gray, his eyes narrowed and imprisoned by deep wrinkles that radiated from the outer corners of his eyes, down and across his cheeks. The third man was heavy-set, with unsmiling dark eyes and hair that sprang from his skull like tumbleweed momentarily at rest. Takawsu recognized the leader of the group at once, for Noble Loomis was well known to the Lenni Lenape; he had often announced coolly that Indians were no better than wild animals and he had killed his share of both.

As the men drew closer, Ahtu bounded forward, a seething mass of concentrated hate. Instantly Loomis raised his rifle to fire. Before Takawsu was aware of her presence, Chilili, who had followed Ahtu from the cabin, leaped forward and seized the wolf, burying her fingers in the fur at the nape of Ahtu's neck.

"No," she shouted at Loomis. "Do not shoot."

"Make sure that critter don't so much as move a muscle," Loomis warned, "or I'll put a hole in it you can walk through."

"No!" Chilili cried again. Takawsu started toward his sister. "Don't move," Loomis said sharply, "because I'd as leave shoot me a couple of Indians as an animal."

"Can't you tell the difference, Noble?" the gray-haired man called out, and guffawed. He was holding a whip and handcuffs. Takawsu had seen whips and handcuffs once before; the man who carried them was a Southern slavedriver searching the area for runaway slaves.

"Well, now you mention it," Loomis answered, "I don't expect I can."

"Go inside, little sister." Takawsu gestured to Chilili.

Loomis' rifle motioned her back. "She can't rightly do that," he insisted, his voice soft. "You there, *sister*," he repeated mockingly. "You come

right on over to me, nice and easy, hear? And you"
— he swiveled his rifle to aim it at Takawsu again
— "hang on to that animal and make sure it don't
move one hair on its head." Unwillingly Chilili
stepped closer. "That's it," Loomis said approvingly, "nice and easy, just like I said, and maybe nobody will get hurt. Tom!" Loomis singled out the
youngest man in the group, a large gawky boy, with
fair hair that seemed almost silver and flat, expressionless, pale blue eyes rimmed with lashes so white
they gave his lids a barren look. "Now, Tom,"
Loomis continued, when the younger man stood
beside him, "I want you to make sure this little girl
don't get no notions whilst I'm palaverin', hear?"

Tom dug his long fingers into Chilili's arm.
"Now you stand here real quiet and good," he cautioned Chilili in his flat colorless voice, "because
Pa's got something he's gonna take care of right
now." He dug his fingers harder. Chilili winced;
Takawsu began to move forward. Instantly a knife
flashed in Tom's hand and was at Chilili's throat.
"You take one more step and you've got one very
dead sister," Tom Loomis said in the tone of a man
who has had to repeat a warning once too often.
"Now you just do as I say. Call that nigger, nice
and loud, just his name. And no tricks. Because I
know Jesse ain't home. We know for a fact he's
still in Corydon. That's why we came now. No

59

sense getting Jesse all riled up, is there? So just go on now, call that nigger out, just like I said."

"No, Takawsu," Chilili called. The knife flicked gently down her cheek and several drops of blood welled up quickly from the nick. Takawsu looked at Tom, his hands frozen in Ahtu's mane. "Someday I shall cut the heart from your body and give it to the dogs to play with till it rots," Takawsu promised quietly. Loomis made an impatient gesture with his rifle. Takawsu turned and faced the cabin. "Sakkaape!"

"Louder!" Loomis whispered.

"Sakkaape!"

Inside the cabin, Sakkaape said urgently to Mekinges, "You know how Jesse Benton loves this land. He will never leave it. Never. Not for you. Not even for the children. Do not make up your mind yet. There is still time before the Lenni Lenape must go."

Mekinges looked down at her hands, folded tightly before her on the rough surface of the small wooden table. "Takawsu grows impatient. Go. I will not make my decision yet. Go," she said with sudden anger. "Do you not hear him calling, again and again?"

"Tell the boy's father Takawsu goes with me. We will bring meat for the table when we return."

Mekinges picked up the moccasin she had

dropped restlessly a moment ago. She began to sew a beaded design of flowers and leaves; even sitting, she gave the impression of grace in movement. Her large eyes were brilliantly dark; her long black hair hung in braids over her shoulders; from her delicately shaped ears hung dangling silver hooped earrings; around her neck she wore rows of shell and bone beads.

"I will tell him," she replied. "But if you wait, you can tell him yourself. He is still in Corydon. But he was certain that he would be back early this day."

"Sakkaape!" The call came again, louder, a little more urgent.

Sakkaape smiled briefly at Mekinges and stepped through the doorway.

"Well now," Loomis greeted him pleasantly. "Look what we have here."

"Looks like we caught ourselves a nigger, Pa, don't it?" Tom said flatly.

"It purely does, son," Loomis agreed. "Now you lay your rifle down, black boy, and move real careful, and maybe we'll let them two go."

Sakkaape stared at Loomis, then put his rifle down carefully. "I am not a runaway slave. You know that." His hand flew to the silver disk. "These men with you, they know it, too."

"My, he sure talks fancy, don't he?" The gray-

61

haired man moved behind Sakkaape and expertly pinioned Sakkaape's hands behind him, snapping the handcuffs around Sakkaape's wrists.

"You've got what you came for," Sakkaape said. "Let the girl go."

"Why sure," Loomis agreed instantly. "Nobody can say I ain't a man of my word. Let the girl go, Tom."

The boy stared sullenly at his father. He sheathed his knife but maintained his grasp on Chilili's arm. Loomis turned and moved menacingly toward his son. "Now, Tom," he said, so quietly it was almost a whisper, "you're riling me. I said let her go."

"I could take good care a this one." Tom's lips set stubbornly. Loomis was now at Tom's side. He swept his arm in a wide swinging arc, the back of his hand landing smartly on the young man's face.

"You just got to listen to me when I talk, Tom," Loomis said reasonably. "Because I ain't got all the patience in the world. Now you know how I get when I'm plumb out of patience. Let her go."

Tom hurled Chilili forward so violently she stumbled and fell at Takawsu's feet. Ahtu snarled, but Takawsu held her firmly. Overhead a cardinal swooped down from the branch of a tree to the roof of the cabin. He emitted an imperative call — two long staccato whistles followed immediately

by four short, sharp reprimands — *chuh, chuh, chuh, chuh*. Almost instantly there came an answering call from behind the four men. Chilili's eyes warmed; Takawsu gave her a warning look.

Loomis pushed Sakkaape before him.

"Wait a minute," Loomis said. He reached over and pulled the silver chain and disk from Sakkaape's neck. "You don't need this anymore. I'll take good care of it for you."

"Come on, Noble," the heavy-set man said uneasily, as the cardinals exchanged another round of calls. "We got what we came for. Let's get out of here."

"What's the all-fired hurry?" a voice from behind the men drawled pleasantly. A tall, rangy man was leaning against a tree, his posture relaxed, his deep blue eyes smiling, his expression blandly interested. "Going somewhere, Noble?" Jesse inquired. His tone seemed neighborly, but his rifle held Loomis squarely at dead reckoning. "Tell your friends to drop their guns," Jesse went on, as if he and Loomis were exchanging pleasantries, "or I'll be obliged to shoot you, Noble, right between the eyes."

"You can't cover four of us at once, Jesse," Noble baited.

"Never for a minute said I could," Benton replied mildly. "But you might try looking behind you." Noble Loomis wheeled about quickly to find himself staring into the muzzle of the gun Mekinges was holding from her stance on the step of the trading post. Noble dropped his rifle. "Do as he says," he commanded the others.

"I ain't going nowhere without this nigger," the gray-haired man muttered. "A squaw and a nigger lover can't stop me." He lifted his rifle. Simultaneously Takawsu released Ahtu, who leaped in a long sinuous movement and felled the man, shrieking in terror and shock, to the ground. At the same moment, Takawsu hurled himself at Tom, wrestling the other until he was pinned to the earth beneath him. Takawsu scooped up a handful of soil and ground it in the other's face.

"You are dirt," Takawsu said through his teeth. "Now I wash your face in it. Another time I will bury you in it." He rose, taking Tom's rifle and knife, and motioned him to join his father, who stood watching the proceedings as if he were a guest at a specially produced performance.

"Ahtu!" Chilili called. The wolf ignored the command. *"Ahtu!"* The girl ran and dragged the animal from the bleeding man, who rose and staggered to stand beside Loomis.

"All right, Noble," Jesse suggested, "get the key and open those chains."

Noble shook his head sadly. "A man that's lived

65

with Indians all his life, it ain't no surprise to me he comes up a nigger lover, too. No surprise a-tall. Somebody really ought to learn you better, Jesse," he said reflectively. "That's a fact."

"Thought you were in a hurry to get somewhere, Noble," Jesse hinted politely.

"I came here nice and legal, Jesse," Noble warned. "I have got me a little handbill describing a runaway slave that fits him" — he waved a hand toward Sakkaape, who still stood chained — "to a T, you might say. There's a reward of two hundred dollars if I fetch him back to Kentucky. And Tom and me, we got big plans for that money."

"It must have cost you a small fortune, getting those handbills printed," Jesse commiserated.

"You've got to spend it to make it." Loomis grinned. He removed the keys from the pocket of the man whom Ahtu had mauled, approached Sakkaape, and released the chains. "You're free, boy, just like you claim. But you know and I know, you were born a slave and you'll die a slave. Free!" He curled his lip. "Let me tell you something . . ." He moved closer to Sakkaape, his pale eyes filled with rage. "I got a pure hankerin' to get you that won't hardly let me be. It's eatin' my gut out, and that's a fact." Loomis turned back to Benton. He looked at the weapons which Takawsu had collected from the men and piled at his father's feet. "You got your nigger back. Now we want our rifles." Jesse shook his head. "You know we can't get on without them rifles," Noble roared. "There's Indians and wild animals in those woods."

"Oh you'll do fine," Jesse reassured him. "From what I hear, vultures always do real well." He moved up to stand beside Loomis. Continuing to use his deceptively friendly tone, he went on, "You show your face around here again, Noble, and I'll nail your hide to the wall."

Sakkaape rubbed his wrists. His hand moved automatically to grasp the silver disk. Benton made a quick gesture with his head. Loomis put his hand in his pocket and dropped the disk on the ground. The men moved off, Tom rubbing the back of his hand across his face, the bleeding man limping and stumbling behind him.

"That man drank poison in his mother's milk," Jesse said reflectively as the men disappeared down the trail. He shrugged his shoulders. "Want to come in and set awhile?" he asked, slapping Sakkaape on the shoulder.

Sakkaape cleaned the silver disk against his trousers.

"Takawsu and I are going back to the trading

post," he said somberly. "We will bring meat when we return."

Benton gave the other man a querying look. "Will you be all right?" he asked.

"I will be all right," Sakkaape replied gravely.

5

———

Takawsu entered *the large building, which was about twenty-five feet wide and sixty feet long, through the door on the north side, along with the others. No one had noticed him, neither when he had joined the men sitting outside the building (the women were also seated in a row outside the building but away from the men) nor now when they had at last arisen to enter. A man and a woman were stationed at the north entrance, another pair at the south door. Inside the fires were already burning; they had been prepared by rubbing two dry sticks together. The fires would be put out and made afresh for each of the twelve days and nights of the meeting, for this was the*

*time of tribal worship, the most solemn conclave of
the year, the conclave that would keep the world
from coming to an end. Everyone sat down, Takawsu with the others. In a moment, Skoligiso,
named for the month of frogs calling, stood, a turtle shell in his hand, the turtle shell filled with pebbles. He stared straight ahead; his hand began to
quiver slowly. At the sound of the pebbles in the
shell, the entire assembly rose. Still staring ahead,
Skoligiso began to speak.*

*"I had a dream in my childhood, a dream of my
brothers, the shooting stars," he began.*

*"He had a dream in his childhood, a dream of
his brothers, the shooting stars," the congregation
chanted in unison.*

*"First I heard a great wind. The wind cried and
I looked up . . ."*

*"First he heard a great wind. The wind cried
and he looked up . . ."*

*"My brother, the shooting star, was shaped like a
head, dripping fire and blood from his mouth, dripping, dripping, dripping . . ."*

*The congregation repeated each word solemnly,
mournfully: ". . . dripping, dripping, dripping . . ."*

*Takawsu repeated the words, too. He ran his
tongue over his lips; he could feel a tremor run
through his body. Shooting stars were brothers to*

the Indians; when they fell, it was because they had been surprised in a lie, in some deceit; rejected and scorned by their brothers, they fled from the sky to seek safe harbor elsewhere. Skoligiso's dream threatened him; he felt it. He folded his hands tightly together to keep them from trembling.

Soon Skoligiso would begin to sing and a group seated apart from the others would echo Skoligiso's words; they would beat upon deerskins pulled taut across four sticks, softly, softly . . . But Skoligiso was not singing; he was staring fixedly at Takawsu, singling him out from the others, maintaining the utmost stillness in posture. Now the entire congregation had turned, they too regarding him silently. All waited. The silence pressed in upon Takawsu, smothering him. Suddenly a strange figure approached, his face and body secreted beneath bearskins, the grotesque head waving, the teeth bared in a snarl, a long stick clutched in the paws and pointing directly at Takawsu. "Leave this place," came a muffled command. "You do not belong."

"Leave this place." The congregation rose, shuffled toward him, slowly, implacably.

Skoligiso began to shake the turtle shell once more. The sound of the pebbles grew louder, more violent . . . still the Indians came . . . closer, closer . . . their movements whispered away into mist, their steps grew sluggish but greater; their

71

*arms reached out to seize him . . . reaching, reach-
ing . . .*

Takawsu's eyes flew open. He sat up, staring wildly
around the room. The meeting house was gone; he
was back in his own home, on his own pallet of
straw in the loft. In the moonlight filtering
through the cracks in the walls, he could see Chilili
curled up on her straw mattress on the rough
wooden planks, serenely asleep, her hand cupped
beneath her chin. Her dark lashes quivered slightly
as she too dreamed, perhaps of her three-legged
fawn, sleeping peacefully with Ahtu, the foster
mother, nearby. So . . . it had been a dream. But
it had terrified him. Even now the echo of the pebbles in the turtle shell reached his ears. Takawsu
shook his head. This was a powerful dream indeed,
for he was awake, wide awake, and yet the clinking
sound persisted. Realization came suddenly. It
was not Skoligiso he heard after all; the muffled
sound came from below. Jesse's chest of silver!

Takawsu slipped from his bed and crossed the
attic stealthily. Chilili turned and mumbled but
did not waken. Before Takawsu descended the
rough wooden ladder leading down to the cabin
below, he kneeled and peered into the darkness,
but he saw nothing and heard nothing. He put his
foot on the first rung and then the next and the

72

next. The silence eddied about him; to Takawsu's straining ears the stillness was deafening. Now, scanning the cabin, he caught a glimpse . . . a shadow mingling with shadows. Mekinges lay sleeping soundly on the bed which was nailed to the south corner of the cabin. Jesse was not in bed; Takawsu wondered fleetingly at his absence. He stepped from the last rung to the cabin floor like a wraith; the intruder did not lift his head. He was intent upon the contents of Jesse's silver chest, filling a deerskin pouch quickly but quietly, removing each piece from the chest and placing it within the pouch with deft movements. A piece of silver slipped from his hand and fell back into the chest with a faint clink; the intruder whipped his head around quickly, one hand flying instantly to the knife at his waist. Turning to inspect the cabin, his glance riveted upon Takawsu.

"Stone Eater!" Takawsu whispered.

In a flash, Stone Eater had moved to the bed and placed his knife to Mekinges' throat.

"One cry and she dies." Stone Eater's eyes burned in the darkness. Takawsu stood motionless. Slowly Stone Eater retreated from the bed toward the door, knife still in hand. Takawsu regarded the other with contempt.

"Once you called the Lenni Lenape women and children," he taunted Stone Eater in a whisper.

"They do not steal. Only the brave warrior who fights women and children comes in the dark, not like a panther leaping on its prey, but like a serpent sliding on the ground."

"I do not need children to lecture me," Stone Eater returned sharply. "I have great need for this money. The Lenni Lenape will go, will leave their lands to the white man, will move like sheep wherever the Kichikani-Yankwis send them. Not so Stone Eater. Stone Eater steals money, yes, to buy many rifles. Then let us see who will move Stone Eater and his braves from the Wapahani and the other lands that are ours."

"A good cause." Jesse's voice startled both Stone Eater and Takawsu. "Don't move," he cautioned as Stone Eater stepped toward him, knife in hand, "because if you do I'll be obliged to use this." He motioned with his rifle.

Mekinges sat up in bed. "He would have killed me for the money," she said flatly.

"You would be better dead." Stone Eater spat at her with contempt. "You have betrayed your people. You have spawned white children . . ."

"I am grandson to a chief," Takawsu cried.

"You are nothing," Stone Eater replied. "You are not Indian. And you are not white. You are nothing!"

Takawsu pressed his lips together angrily. Jesse

cautioned, "My son, he is a man possessed. You cannot argue with him." He turned to the other. "Just throw that pouch down, nice and easy . . ."

"The pouch is mine."

"Fancy that," Jesse said drily. Stone Eater hurled the pouch at Takawsu's feet.

"What is it? What is happening?" Chilili's voice was rimmed with sleep. Her feet appeared on the ladder as she spoke. Jesse turned and looked up; in a flash of movement, Stone Eater was through the door of the cabin and lost in the darkness outside.

"He's getting away!" Takawsu cried. "We must go after him."

"*Listen!*" Chilili called. She was suddenly wide awake and apprehensive. "*Listen!*"

The silence in the cabin was pierced by a terrified bleating cry.

"It is nothing," Jesse said after a moment. "I heard it before and went out to look. Wolves are hunting."

"No!" Chilili exclaimed. "It is Maskanako!" She went rushing from the cabin.

"Wait. Chilili. Wait," Jesse called. But it was too late; Chilili was already running swiftly to the pen where the fawn was kept. Jesse followed as swiftly; behind him Takawsu and Mekinges were close on his heels.

75

"Look!" Chilili's command was unnecessary. They had all seen the wolf in the enclosure, all heard the fawn shrilling his terror into the darkness that surrounded him. Jesse raised his rifle but Mekinges struck it down.

"No," she warned, for at the moment Jesse took aim Ahtu came hurtling across the ground, leaping up and over the fence, her slanting eyes gleaming yellow in the moonlight, her teeth bared, snarling, murderous, to rescue her young from the marauder. The intruder leaped to the attack; with a chilling cry he turned from the frightened deer to close in on Ahtu. The two wolves tore at each other with their teeth, rolling and twisting on the ground.

"Stop them. Stop them," Chilili begged tearfully. Jesse raised his rifle once more, then dropped it to his side again.

"I can't shoot," he said helplessly. "I can't take the risk of killing Ahtu."

Chilili, watching, wrung her hands. Takawsu urged Ahtu on, hardly aware of his words. "Fight, my brave one," he whispered. "The Great Spirit is within you. Fight, Ahtu. Your name is honored. It will be preserved for all time."

Momentarily, the wolves separated. Grasping the opportunity, Jesse aimed and fired. Ahtu howled, a long smooth cry that filled Chilili's heart with dread.

76

"You have killed Ahtu," she sobbed, her eyes blinded with tears.

"No, my daughter," Mekinges said gently. "Look. It is not Ahtu who lies so still."

Chilili ran to the gate, opened it, and sped into the pen. Ahtu lay moaning on the ground, panting. Chilili dropped to her side and began to stroke the wolf's head, her tears falling softly on the animal's face. "Ahtu is bleeding" — she lifted her head at Jesse's step — "she is hurt." Jesse kneeled beside her and examined Ahtu's wounds.

"She is hurt," he agreed, "but she will not die. Your mother will help you care for her." He glanced up at Mekinges, who nodded. "Look," Jesse said softly, touching Chilili's face and lifting it from its downcast position. "See who else will help you care for Ahtu."

Chilili raised her head. A smile trembled on her lips. Maskanako had approached. Timidly he surveyed the humans. Then gently and lovingly, he bent his head to Ahtu and began to lick her wounds.

6

————

IT WAS JULY — Yaukāūtamwaa Kēēshooh — the time of feast of first fruits. Early in the month, the Lenni Lenape had witnessed a strange ceremony, a day of celebration among the white settlers who had come to the area within the past six months. Fourth of July the white men had called it, and they had asked the Lenni Lenape to join the festivities. Pride Finch had been there, and Isaac Hamaker, who had built the mill, the Curtises, the Wilsons, and the Jennings family, who had traveled west with thirteen children and lost all but three to the smallpox epidemic that had claimed lives from every settler's cabin. The Lenni Lenape had come and watched the proceedings silently.

Jesse stood a little apart from the others. Calling for the attention of those who had assembled, he said gravely, "This is our first Fourth of July. Nothing any of us could say could be more solemn, more fitting to this occasion than these words." Quietly at first, and then with growing emphasis, Jesse began to recite.

When in the course of human events, it becomes necessary for one people to dissolve the political bands which have connected them with another, and to assume among the powers of the earth, the separate and equal station to which the Laws of Nature and of Nature's God entitle them, a decent respect to the opinions of mankind requires that they should declare the causes which impel them to the separation.

We hold these truths to be self-evident, that all men are created equal, that they are endowed by their Creator with certain unalienable Rights, that among these are Life, Liberty and the pursuit of Happiness . . .

The words eddied across the open fields. The settlers listened intently, seriously absorbed as if in church; the Lenni Lenape sat in a semicircle outside the group of whites, faces blank, eyes expressionless. Sakkaape stood to one side, arms folded, with no flicker of emotion, his eyes as impassive as those of the Delaware Indians.

When at last Jesse finished speaking, there was a long moment of silence. Then Pride Finch broke from the group to drive forks of wood briskly into the ground, across which the Hamaker boys laid poles. Then they helped the two Jennings boys cover the poles with brush. The Jennings girl along with the other women and girls brought generous portions of food into the shade of the newly built shelter. Jesse, his eyes sparkling with excitement, had offered the first toast. "To America," he cried.

"To America," the men roared, and drank.

"To our first Fourth of July celebration," Jesse then proposed. His sentiments were vigorously endorsed.

Pride Finch had exchanged glances with Elizabeth Jennings, his homely face beaming. She raised her brows and gave him a small meaningful nod. Instantly Finch broke into the uproar with a bellow for silence. When he had everyone's attention, he muttered, "I guess it's no secret I've been courting Miss Elizabeth."

"Louder, Finch, louder," someone shouted.

"Well, she's done me the great honor . . ."

"Louder. Louder," someone else cried out. "Ain't nothing you're ashamed of!"

"We're getting married!" Finch roared. "And everyone here is asked to the wedding!"

Jesse joined Mekinges, sitting with her people on the periphery of the shelter. Chilili, beside her mother, looked up at Jesse's approach.

"What is a wedding?" she asked.

Jesse grinned down at her. "It is a ceremony at which a husband takes a wife."

Chilili glanced at Mekinges. "Did Mekinges my mother have a wedding?" she asked with interest.

For the first time since she had come to the Fourth of July picnic, Mekinges smiled at her husband. "It is different among our people," she answered Chilili.

Jesse and Mekinges, smiling at each other over their daughter's head, remembered how it had been with them. Jesse had been well known in the Delaware camp; he could slip in and out of the village like one of them. He had seemed not to pay attention to Mekinges, but she had known that his eyes followed her every move. When she would go to the river, he would contrive to be there; he would invent excuses to consult with Mekinges' father and whenever he had come to the cabin, he had brought her gifts, and gifts to the chief as well.

One day Mekinges had come to the trading post with the others, with Winikiso, her brother, M'chakhocque, named for the month when the cold makes the trees crack, the Mamhotin, who was like the month in which he was born — the hungry month — always looking for something to eat. They had brought their furs to the trading post, but the trader had not paid close attention to the skins, for which oversight Mekinges later chided

Jesse; Mamhotin was not above tucking a piece of stone or metal between the skins to add to the weight of the furs. If confronted with an accusation of cheating, he would blandly deny knowledge of the attempted deception and just as blandly try the same trickery the next time he appeared at the post. When their business had been transacted, the men had left the cabin. Jesse had caught Mekinges by the hand as she too turned to leave.

"Do not go," Jesse had said in a low voice.

Mekinges' heart had leaped within her; it had taken him so long to speak! She had not replied, but from that moment on the trading post had been her home.

The sound of their daughter's voice brought Mekinges and Jesse back to the present. "Will we go to the wedding?" Chilili was saying persistently.

"If you wish it," Jesse promised.

As it turned out, Chilili did not even have to leave home to attend the ceremony, for Jesse had offered his grounds for the affair. Elizabeth Jennings, her wedding dress wrapped in a sack, had gone to the smokehouse to change into her finery, a white dress her mother had worn, the lace at its neck and wrists yellowing but delicate. The ceremony had been planned to take place inside the trading post, but the day was too lovely for the wedding to take place indoors, Elizabeth said.

Agreeably, the neighbors gathered in the field, the men in their buckskin pants and vests, the women in their homespun clothes, blues and browns predominating, the ruffles around their necks and the ribbons which held their calico bonnets close on their heads ruffling in the gentle summer breeze. Beyond the intimate circle of Elizabeth and Pride Finch, the circuit-riding minister, and the ring of interested neighbors, the Lenni Lenape stood and watched, their faces impassive, their eyes silently absorbing the strange scene. Mekinges, too, had withdrawn from the settlers, choosing to remain with her people on the periphery of activity.

"Do you, Pride Finch, take Elizabeth Jennings . . ." The words drifted across the meadow, familiar and pleasing to the ears of the settlers, incomprehensible to the Lenni Lenape. Ceremonies they understood, for they had many of their own — for the hunt, for supplication to Manito, the Great Spirit, for curing the ill — but this taking of a wife and the endless stream of words were puzzling. Where were the gifts for the parents of the bride? It was over at last; the women swarmed about the bride, bussing her on either cheek, while the men pounded Finch on the back and broke into loud guffaws as one or another made low-voiced, meaningful suggestions to the perspiring groom.

Now the feasting began, and this the Delaware Indians understood well. In the middle of a long wooden table a fine saddle of venison steamed succulently, flanked on each side with large, beautifully plump wild turkeys, roasted and still hot from the clay oven in which they had been baked, and fish freshly caught from the Wapahani; dessert was plentiful, too. Elizabeth had baked some pies; the other women had brought wild apples and plums preserved in maple sugar, and from a large sugar kettle hanging over the fireplace inside the trading post, Mekinges now dispensed coffee, which the women sweetened with maple sugar and the men with generous tots of whiskey.

Sakkaape, too, present because both Finch and Jesse had insisted, stood near the cabin, apart from the wedding group and the Lenni Lenape, watching the scene in mild amusement. Takawsu came, a turkey leg in his hand, his mouth filled with food. "It is good," he informed Sakkaape. "Aren't you hungry?"

Sakkaape shook his head. "I will eat in a little while."

"This wedding" — Takawsu regarded the turkey leg critically to see if he had missed any meat — "it is a silly thing with the man reading words from a little book, but the food is good." He tossed the

85

bone aside. "I will go and get more. Do you wish me to bring you something?"

Once again Sakkaape shook his head. "Go quickly," he said, smiling, "or it might be gone before you get there."

Grinning, Takawsu moved away toward the still groaning tables. Halfway there, he turned to look back; what he saw arrested him where he stood. "Sakkaape!" he shouted, and sped back; but when he reached the spot where he had left the tall black man, there was no sign of him. Grimly, Takawsu followed the trail and then, taking stock of the situation that confronted him, retraced his steps.

The Lenni Lenape, having feasted, had meanwhile dispersed; the bride and groom had made their way down the hill toward the river, where Finch had handed his bride into a canoe and then joined her, to begin paddling across the quiet water to the cabin he had built on the other side. Jesse stood laughing when the sound of Takawsu's voice reached him. Finch held the paddle steady so the canoe remained close to shore.

"What is it?" Jesse asked sharply, his eyes alert.

"Sakkaape!" Takawsu blurted breathlessly. "They've taken him. I saw it. I followed and then came back to tell you. They've taken him."

"Who?" Jesse said quietly.

"Noble Loomis. He and the others. They came

behind Sakkaape and took him while everyone was busy with the feast."

Finch paddled the canoe back to shore.

"What are you doing?" his new wife demanded.

Finch stared at her in surprise.

"Why, I'm going to help Jesse find Sakkaape and bring him back," he replied reasonably.

"This is my wedding day!" Elizabeth's face turned crimson with anger.

"Well it's my wedding day too," Finch bellowed, "but I figure it will keep awhile. I'm not sure I can say the same about Noble Loomis and that's a fact, Mrs. Finch." He thrust the paddle into her hands and leaped ashore. Elizabeth pressed her lips together. She was "sore as a boil," Finch confessed ruefully as he joined Jesse, who was moving swiftly back to the trading post to pick up his rifle. Elizabeth seized the paddle in an iron grip and began to move the canoe furiously across the river to the cabin she had fully counted upon to enter expectantly with her new husband.

Isaac Hamaker, who had been about to leave, addressed his wife, who had piled the children into the wagon preparatory to making the long trip home. "Now don't get in a fret, Rebeccah," he advised her, "if I don't get home for a spell. I've got to give Jesse a hand and help pin back Noble Loomis' ears."

Rebeccah nodded. "You give him hail Columbia," she said crisply, snapping the reins sharply. "Him and that Tom. You stay with it till the cows come home if you have to," she shouted back as the wagon moved off.

Jesse, of the three men ready to hunt down the kidnapers, was the only one who had been born and bred in the wilderness; his eyes could assess and interpret every inch of the land. With Takawsu at his side, Jesse led the others as sure-footedly as if the trail had been blazed for them with markers.

"They did not even trouble to cover their tracks," Takawsu said scornfully.

Jesse nodded, his searching glance scanning the ground around him. "Loomis is a bigger fool than I suspected," he muttered at last. "He's heading for the rough."

"The rough?" Finch echoed, puzzled. Although he had settled in the area months ago, it was rare for him to leave the smithy.

"The hazel rough," Hamaker broke in. "That's that stretch of land to the south. No timber on it," he explained to Finch. But it was mean country, nevertheless, a matted, tangled jungle of hazel brush lashed together with grape vines, impossible to settle, poor land for men but fine protection for wild animals.

"Sounds like a good place for a man to hide," Finch said.

"No," Jesse said shortly. "It's wild hog country . . . those hogs are dangerous and mean. I'd sooner tangle with panthers."

When they reached the thicket, the men dismounted. "Stay here," Jesse advised them. "I'm going in for a look." Cautiously he crept into the brush, sliding in under the tangle. Before long, however, he emerged to warn the others to retreat. "There's a nest of young pigs in there," Jesse whispered. "We'd better leave before they start squealing. Once they do . . ." He stopped and listened. "On your horses," he snapped. "I can hear hogs coming at us from every direction."

"I'm not afraid of a *hog*," Finch started to protest.

"*Ride!*" Jesse shouted, but his command came too late, for out of the thicket a group of savage hogs seemed to attack from every side. One hog singled out Finch's horse. The horse screamed and reared as the tusk gored him; startled, Finch lost his seat and fell. Instantly the hog veered toward him. Jesse's rifle exploded; the bullet tore into the hog but the impact of his charge was so violent it carried him on and over Finch before he fell dead at Finch's outflung arm. The other rifles were spitting

89

now; Takawsu and Hamaker kept up a continuous bellowing to frighten away the enraged swine; the furor was deafening but eventually successful, for at last the hogs retreated into the thicket from which they had emerged in defense of their territory. Finch rose to his feet, pale and shaken by the experience, and examined his horse; muttering, he drew the wounded animal to one side. The others waited for the sound of the shot; they knew the horse was so seriously injured it had to be destroyed — knew, too, what a grievous moment this was for the gentle Finch.

"Are you all right?" Jesse asked when at last Finch rejoined the others, his face set, his eyes curiously blank. Finch made a slight gesture with his hand. "Then we'll go on," Jesse said quietly. Catching the bridle of his horse, Jesse turned and led the way, the others following silently in his footsteps. Now the trail led north again and east toward the headwaters of Lick Creek. Hamaker exclaimed, "Loomis must be out of his mind. He's making tracks like a turkey in a fit."

"Most likely trying to confuse whoever's coming after," Finch offered in a hoarse voice. Takawsu turned and stared at the burly blacksmith. Confuse Jesse, who had hunted, fished, trapped in these lands since childhood, who like the Lenni Lenape had traversed north, south, east, and west over this territory tracking game?

The little posse moved on. At last Jesse called a halt. He stood rigid, listening; Takawsu, too, froze, his eyes alert, his head cocked to one side. Hamaker and Finch waited, puzzled. Jesse nodded to Takawsu. Instantly the boy disappeared into the forest, edging his way gingerly toward the creek, toward the faint wailing that ended abruptly even as Takawsu was sickening at what his eyes beheld. As silently as he had come he backtracked to where he had left Jesse and the others; motioning them to fall in behind him, he raced back to the creek.

Inured as he was to the brutalities of frontier living, even Jesse could not stomach what they found. Hamaker clenched his rifle grimly; only Finch spoke out in horror. "My God," he cried, "it's a bloody massacre!"

"Let's go in there and get those murdering animals!" Hamaker muttered at last, starting forward.

Jesse put a restraining hand on Hamaker's arm. "We want them alive," he warned.

"After what they just did," Finch exploded. "I'd as soon take those wild hogs . . ."

"Alive and unharmed." Jesse was firm. "We'll take them back to Bentonville and see that they stand trial."

"If the Indians don't get them first," Hamaker said with satisfaction. "Look there, Jesse!"

"Stone Eater!" Takawsu cried.

"Quick," Jesse shouted, and pounded into the clearing. The others were hard on his heels.

7

THE NEW COURTHOUSE had been thrown together in great haste for the trial. The log building was about twenty by thirty feet and boasted a strong puncheon floor. At the far end of the room a three-foot-high platform had been erected on which a bench had been placed for the circuit court judge and the two side judges, together with a rough wooden table at which the court clerk would sit and note the proceedings as best he could. A railing separated the judges from the bench which would serve counsel. Not far from this bench a small enclosure had been placed which would hold the prisoner. To one side of the room stood another smaller bench which had been readied for the witnesses. Hiram Winchell, the sheriff, had judiciously positioned a long pole between the participants and the crowd that would presently flow into the courtroom.

Outside, the crowd had already begun to gather, despite the heat which made them already moist and clammy under the blazing August sun. Some had come from as far off as the Ohio line to the east; others had traveled for days from the Michigan boundary. A feeling of camaraderie and festivity filled the air, for though the crime was murder and feelings ran high both for and against the prisoner, coming to hear the lawyers plead was more exciting than a shooting match, more fun than a chivaree, and considerably more interesting than either a wedding or a funeral. The event had drawn a number of itinerant preachers, each of whom was exhorting in his own fashion the jostling groups gathered to listen to the Word of the Lord as translated by the self-appointed bringers of the Word. And the exhortations, too, were biased, depending upon which way the preachers' views blew.

"And I say unto you, that many shall come from the East and West, and shall sit down with Abraham, Isaac, and Jacob, in the kingdom of heaven," proclaimed a small fair man, his light blue eyes bulging under disappearing brows, as he mopped his face which dripped from heat and fervor intermingled. "Yes, they shall come from the East and the West, from the North and the South, from every part of the globe where man ever lived, or died — of every color, nation, kingdom — of every sect, of every tongue, from every congregation, from every people . . ."

"Hey, Reverend," shouted an irreverent voice from the crowd. "You telling us we're gonna find Indians in heaven, same as us?" A sweep of laughter greeted his outburst. The small man turned upon the heckler with wrath. "I'm telling you, I'm telling all of you," he cried, "that whoever comes before the Lord with a pure heart and a contrite spirit — even you, my friend" — he pointed a shaking finger — "should I meet such a one — whatever his color, be he Indian or white, then I would feel like the mariner at sea, in a dark night, when his foundering vessel is tempest tossed; he casts his eye above and if he sees one twinkling star peering through the darkness, he hails it with a thousand times more joy than he would on a clear night the whole galaxy of the heavens overspread."

The preacher closed his eyes, overcome with emotion. A few women in the crowd touched bits of cambric to their eyes. Indians in heaven were a totally preposterous idea, of course, but the reverend did make a nice speech. It pleasured them to hear him.

Takawsu, who had lingered behind Jesse, had listened open-mouthed at the fluency of the exhortations, going from one group to another, finding the whole scene alien and strange. Not so did the Lenni Lenape mete out justice. The atmosphere reminded him somehow of the celebration last month which the white people had called the Fourth of July. Racing to catch up with Jesse, Takawsu headed for the courthouse. Over the din of laughter and conversation Takawsu heard Hiram Winchell's voice bellowing out the names of the jurors, a clarion call to arms that turned the crowd away from the men of the cloth to the log building and the moment they had long awaited.

The presiding judge was Harvey Sweetz, judge of the Third Judicial Circuit of the State of Indiana. His jurisdiction cut a huge swath of territory, from Jefferson County in the south sweeping two hundred miles north to the Michigan line, from Ohio to the east as far west as the White River. Whether it was due to the constant journeying across land still sparsely settled to sit court in villages where Indians outnumbered the frontiersmen or the nature of the cases that came before him, Judge Sweetz, unlike the implication of his name, was an irascible, short-tempered man. In an area where men were commonly hardy and frequently tall, the judge towered, for he was literally a giant in size, with an extraordinarily huge head and broad muscular chest. His features were prominent under a wide, high forehead, in which, when the judge was irritated beyond endurance, a large vein pulsed angrily.

The crowd, having filtered into the courtroom and stuffed it to capacity, was still in holiday mood, jostling and laughing and calling out to each other across the room. When Judge Sweetz entered, he swept the courtroom with so fiery a gaze from his brilliantly dark morose eyes that an unaccustomed silence fell on the assemblage at once. Without a word, the judge seated himself upon the bench. Behind him came Rufus Taney, who ran the grist-mill, and Moses Wick, who had but recently built a tavern in the new village named Bentonville. Neither Taney nor Wick had any clear notion of the law; Wick could barely write his name; Taney was not even this fully qualified for he was totally illiterate. But neither man felt himself handicapped. In fact, Taney had been chosen as one of the side judges (both men had been selected by the people of the community for this task, as was the custom in the early days of the traveling court) because of his frequent boast that he had been sued so many times he knew at least as much about the law as the next man.

As soon as Judge Sweetz was seated, a young

man rose from the lawyers' bench and addressed the court. Before entering the courtroom, Russell Stopping, who was representing the prisoner, had carefully removed his rorum hat, stiffened with glue to keep its shape, from the back of which a three-foot queue, tied from one end to another with an eel skin, dangled elegantly. Without the hat perched on his head, the young man felt somewhat insecure. Consequently when he spoke to the judges, he clutched the hat nervously in his hands.

"Your Honor — Your Honors," he amended, "the two gentlemen beside me" — he indicated the bench on which two men sat eagerly eyeing the judicial bench — "would like to be admitted to this bar for the duration of this trial as attorneys and counselors. They are lawyers from Ohio."

Judge Sweetz glared at Russell, but when he spoke it was mildly enough. "I presume they have come here to defend the prisoners."

"Yes, Your Honor."

"Let them serve," Taney roared.

Judge Sweetz compressed his lips. "And I assume these gentlemen are lawyers in the state of Ohio?"

"They have not brought their licenses with them," Russell replied anxiously, "but they are regular practitioners in law."

"Of course they are." The irrepressible Taney

guffawed. "Nobody but a lawyer would defend a murderer."

"We don't know, Mr. Taney," Judge Sweetz said sharply, "that the defendant is a murderer until it has been so proved in this court."

Taney subsided. Even he quailed under the judge's fierce stare.

Russell returned to the bench for counsel and held a hurried consultation in low tones with his colleagues, after which he once again returned to speak to the judges.

"I move the court grant a writ of habeas corpus, to bring up the prisoners, that is, the first prisoner to come before this court, Your Honor, now being illegally confined in the jail."

"For *what?*" Moses Wick spoke up for the first time since he had seated himself beside Judge Sweetz.

"A writ of habeas corpus." Russell's lips quirked in a near smile.

"What do you do with it?" Moses asked curiously.

"I want to bring up the prisoner I am defending and have him discharged."

"Can he do that?" Moses asked ingenuously of Judge Sweetz. "Is there any law for that?"

"It is a constitutional writ," Judge Sweetz allowed.

"Well, constitutional or not," came a voice from the bench where the witnesses had convened, "nobody is going to take those irons off Loomis. I put them on and I'll take them off. But not until he's stood trial, habeas corpus or no habeas corpus." It was Pride Finch who had spoken, enraged at what he felt were typical lawyer shenanigans. He had warned Jesse darkly about this when Jesse had insisted on a trial for Loomis.

Judge Sweetz turned and glared at the burly blacksmith. "I make the decisions here," he barked. "The witness will sit down and will hold his tongue until he is on the witness stand." The judge swiveled about and regarded the young lawyer without expression. "Motion overruled. Let the jury be impaneled," he instructed Hiram Winchell.

"There's no need to do that," Winchell said happily. "Old Doc Bates made out a list . . ."

"He did what?" the judge roared. "Is Doctor Bates in the courtroom?" A genial-looking man with a shiny bald pate and brown twinkling eyes in a moon-shaped face rose from one of the seats that had been poled off in the room. Sweetz motioned for Winchell to hand him the list and then beckoned the doctor forward to the bench.

"Is this your handwriting?" Judge Sweetz demanded, handing the list of names to the doctor.

"It is," the doctor acknowledged, beaming with pride.

Judge Sweetz leaned forward and impaled the other with a string of words tossed out like a series of flashing knives. "My dear sir, there is no jail that I can put you in, for the present jail is full to overflowing; but it is the judgment of this court . . ."

"I hand-picked those men." The doctor appeared to be shocked that his efforts were being brushed aside.

". . . that you be banished from these hearings until the trial is over. Sheriff! See that the judgment of the court is carried strictly into execution."

"Come along, Doc." Winchell placed a firm hand on the other man's arm.

"It's not fair," the doctor wailed. "I've never been to a real murder trial before."

When the process of choosing the jurors was over, the judge drew a deep breath, advised the jury to retire to Wick's tavern for some sustenance, and announced that the court would reconvene after the noonday meal.

Pride Finch was filled with forebodings, which he confided gloomily to Jesse and Takawsu.

"They'll never try him, not fair that is," he prophesied. "Did you see who's on that jury? Fletcher Cornell!" Finch snorted. "And Simon Harmar."

"He's getting his day in court," Jesse replied

101

tiredly. "Like the judge said, it'll be proved in court that he's a murderer."

Finch subsided unhappily. A peaceful man normally, he boiled with rage whenever he remembered his wedding day and its aftermath. Nor did his anger abate even when Loomis — pale and haggard, a scraggly growth of beard covering his chin, his thin body almost emaciated, and his cavernous eyes sunk deep in their sockets — was brought into court after the recess by Hiram Winchell and two deputies. Loomis was brought before the judges' bench.

"How do you plead?" Judge Sweetz asked.

Loomis raised his head and looked slowly around the courtroom, his glance flicking from one spectator to another, coming to rest at last where Finch sat beside Jesse, Takawsu, Hamaker, and Sakkaape. Pulling his baleful stare at last from Sakkaape's impassive face to the waiting judges, he smiled. "Not guilty."

Judge Sweetz motioned the sheriff to put the prisoner in the pen, then peered at the lawyers. "Is counsel ready?" he asked.

Russell Stopping nodded. "Counsel for the defense is ready, Your Honor."

"Counsel for the prosecution is ready," Benjamin Barbour boomed.

"Call your first witness," the prosecuting attorney was instructed.

Takawsu was sworn in after considerable wrangling, the defense attorney taking the position that Takawsu was half Indian and consequently a prejudiced witness, to which contention Moses Wick remarked with comic candor that everybody in that room was prejudiced one way or another and could they get on with it, because trial or no trial, he had a tavern to run.

"Now, John." Barbour approached Takawsu and lowered his naturally booming voice a decibel. "In your own words, tell this court what you saw . . ."

"It started on Mr. Finch's wedding day," Takawsu began, "when I saw Noble Loomis and his friends kidnap . . ."

"Objection," Stopping leaped to his feet. "This witness is stating his opinion . . ."

"The witness is merely telling what he saw," the prosecuting attorney roared.

Judge Sweetz pounded the table before him with his gavel.

"The Judge wants quiet," Hiram Winchell bellowed.

When Takawsu was able to speak again, he rephrased his statement. He had run to tell Jesse

103

that Sakkaape was gone; they had tracked Loomis and his party to the creek; he had gone ahead, had heard a cry. Takawsu's voice faltered, then gathered momentum. Before his eyes, he had seen Loomis' son Tom pick up a crying Indian child and smash it against a log while Loomis stood by smiling.

"You're an Indian, aren't you?" Russell Stopping asked on cross-examination. "This tribe you belong to, the Delawares, isn't it? They're cannibals, isn't that right?"

"Objection!" Barbour shouted.

"Sustained!" Judge Sweetz glared at the young lawyer. "Even if such a statement were true, the Indians and their customs are not on trial in this courtroom. The boy is a witness, not a criminal. You will not badger him in my court, is that perfectly clear?"

"Give it to him, Judge," Taney said, regarding the young man with contempt. Taney held no brief for the Indians or this half-breed son of Jesse's; on the other hand he had no use for a man who held himself superior because he had a little book learning and a fancy hat.

Pride Finch's testimony followed Takawsu's. Finch, too, somberly relived that moment when he had reached the clearing. Tied to a tree to one side was Sakkaape, the man they had come to rescue.

On the ground lay the bodies of three women, two men, two boys, and two little girls — "no more than ten," Finch said hoarsely. One of the white men in Loomis' party was packing a horse with everything of value they had found in this small Indian camp — the Indians had had some good fortune in trapping and had a quantity of furs — while Loomis and another man were kneeling on the ground — Finch swallowed as his gorge rose once again in the remembrance — mutilating the bodies.

"You did not actually see my client shoot any member of the Indian party?" Stopping asked.

"No, I didn't," Finch answered, "but I saw enough. You want to hear exactly what he did . . ."

"No more questions," Stopping said quickly.

". . . he was kneeling next to this woman . . ."

"I said no more questions," Stopping shouted.

"That will be all, Mr. Finch," Judge Sweetz said sharply. He pulled a large cloth from his pocket and mopped his massive brow. Between the intense heat and the vivid description of the scene in the clearing, his stomach was beginning to heave. He should never have gone to the tavern at the noontime break, he thought morosely; it might, until the witnesses were through testifying, be a splendid idea to forgo eating entirely.

"I call the man known as Sakkaape," the prosecuting attorney requested. Instantly there was an uproar. Russell Stopping was shouting, "Objection! A Negro cannot testify against a white man," while the people in the courtroom broke into a buzz of loud-voiced conversation, pro and con. Russell continued to object, even after the gavel descended and the judge threatened to clear the court.

"There is no color in the eyes of justice," Barbour commented acidly. "Sakkaape is a free man, and an eyewitness from the very beginning . . ."

"No, sir. He is black," Russell said hotly. "Free or not free, you can't put the word of a black man against the word of a white man."

Sweetz pounded his gavel. "I will decide who can testify in this court." His voice shook with rage. "Sheriff, have the man sworn in. And you, sir" — he pointed the gavel menacingly at the defense attorney — "will be good enough to sit down and be quiet!"

Looking straight ahead, speaking in a calm, clear voice, Sakkaape took them back to the day of the wedding. Loomis had come up behind him; prodding Sakkaape roughly in the small of his back with the barrel of his rifle, Loomis had warned him against any outcry. In the excitement, only the boy Takawsu had noticed the kidnaping. It had been a

106

large party; four of the men with Loomis had fled on horses immediately — this was to lead whoever followed (Loomis had assumed and rightly that Jesse would give chase) astray while Loomis, his son Tom, and two other white men hid, watched Jesse and his party take off, and then headed straight for the headwaters of Lick Creek, where Loomis would meet a Southern slavedriver who was to pay $200 for Sakkaape. They had tied Sakkaape to a tree and had then ambushed the small party of Indians, a quiet group who had set up temporary camp near the banks of the creek. Then they had decided to mutilate the bodies to make it appear that it had been the work of other marauding Indians from another tribe. They had been surprised at their macabre task by the arrival of Jesse Benton, Pride Finch, Isaac Hamaker, and the boy Takawsu, Benton's son.

During the recital, the jury appeared to grow uneasy. Fletcher Cornell whittled away relentlessly at a large hickory stick; Simon Harmar, like the rest of the jurors moccasin-shod and wearing a side knife, cleaned his nails with an almost religious devotion to the task, never once raising his glance to look at the witness.

One Indian had escaped at the outset; he had fled to the creek but Loomis had shot him as he reached the water. Nonetheless, before the

wounded man had disappeared from view, Sakkaape had recognized him, for he had turned full
face, his eyes burning with hatred. It had been
Stone Eater, an Indian warrior already dedicated to
avenging his people.

Jesse was last to testify. He corroborated the
stories of the other witnesses. He had also seen
Stone Eater escape, and was therefore not surprised
when later Stone Eater, clutching his left upper
arm where it had been grazed by the shot from
Loomis' gun, reappeared with a group of Indians.
The Indians had demanded that Loomis and the
others be given to them, but Jesse had refused.
Loomis, he assured the Indian party, would be
taken back as a prisoner, along with his partners in
crime, to stand trial for murder.

"No," Stone Eater had sworn. "We know what
the white man's justice is."

Jesse had acknowledged gravely that Stone Eater
had cause to doubt the white man's word, and so
he had turned to another, a chief whose word carried much weight among the braves. "You know
me," he had told the chief. "I have lived among
you as a son and a brother; I am married to a
daughter of your village; you and I speak one
tongue. Do not take matters into your own hands.
I give you my promise, as a son and brother, that
these men will be brought to justice." Stone Eater

had lashed out angrily against the "white son," but the chief had listened to Jesse, reminding him that if the white men were freed, as Stone Eater firmly believed they would be, then the Indian nation would rise and strike as never before in their history.

Summing up, Jesse spoke out against men like Loomis, who warred against black men and red men and before whom no man, whatever his skin or creed, could feel himself secure . . . a man who set himself outside the law, to whom the act of killing brought savage joy.

Loomis' pale eyes never shifted from Jesse's face during Jesse's moments on the witness chair. When at last Jesse stepped down and passed Loomis caged in the pen, Loomis hissed, "You ain't no better than those Indians, Jesse. When I get outta here, you can expect a little visit from me, you and those half-breeds of yourn and that squaw you live with. Yes, sir. I look forward to that day, Jesse. I purely do."

8

RUSSELL STOPPING'S SUMMATION was a master-
piece of eloquent prejudice. Skillfully he drew
blood as he spoke in tones of hushed horror of
early Indian massacres of white men and women
and their families; men on the jury nodded their
heads in grim affirmation as they remembered that
their own lives had been touched with similar trage-
dies. Stopping recalled incidents in the history of
the frontier hero, Daniel Boone, and then swung
into a vivid account of the defeat of General St.
Clair and Harmar at the hands of the marauding
savages. When his voice finally died away on the
last syllable, the crowd in the courtroom cheered.
Noble Loomis stared insolently at Jesse, sitting

tight-lipped near the pole that separated him from the lawyers' bench and the prisoner's pen, then turned and winked at the jury.

Judge Sweetz waited angrily for the furor to subside, then nodded for the prosecuting attorney to begin his summation. Barbour rose and moved slowly to stand before the jury. He pulled a handkerchief from his pocket and mopped his face and the back of his neck. "It is *hot*," he said amiably. He glanced over to where Russell Stopping was whispering with the attorneys from Ohio and added with a grin, "Almost as hot as the defense attorney's speech." Russell responded with the barest hint of an answering smile. He was feeling flushed with victory and could afford to be generous. "All that about Daniel Boone." Barbour shook his head, raised his brows, and half closed his eyes in one continuous movement. "Very well done. Very well done. I was kind of disappointed, though. He never once mentioned George Washington, or even George Rogers Clark. Now a Hoosier hero like Clark should have been brought up even in passing. I'm surprised, Russell, I'm really surprised. Another thing Russell didn't think to bring up was the little matter of justice."

Barbour stepped back to a small table, picked up some clothing, returned to the jury, and shook the clothing at them as his voice became charged with fury. "Look at this, gentlemen. These are the bloody clothes of the victims, cut down without cause or reason. Here. The dress of a five-year-old girl. A savage? A *child!* A group of quiet, inoffensive Indians, fishing and hunting, peacefully camping on the banks of the creek, murdered for a few paltry furs. And if foul murder was not enough, mutilation. Desecration of the dead. Mr. Stopping used the word savages about a hundred times. Who was savage in that clearing?" Barbour's voice shook. "Mr. Stopping told us a lot of things, about frontier hardships and frontier skirmishes. What about frontier justice and the frontier sense of what is right? We live in a wilderness, he said. Agreed. But we are Christians. We know the difference between right and wrong. The laws of this country do not end at some boundary line to the east. Murder is no more justifiable here than it is anywhere in the land. If it is, then no man, no woman, no child is safe."

Barbour paused a moment, turning away from the jury to regard the filled courtroom speculatively.

"Safe," he repeated softly. "There's a word to build a picture in your mind. In this village of Bentonville there are perhaps forty settlers, all told. How many Indians are out there in the wilderness, my friends, biding their time, waiting to see what

the white man means when he speaks of justice before the law? Will they see foul murder approved, and murderers riding free to kill again? If they do, believe me, you will see a blood bath such as has never been witnessed in the land before. For mark my words, they will demand revenge. The Delawares on the White River are leaving Indiana in October. That much is true. But October is still three months away. And not every Indian tribe is moving west. Will they sweep down on this community and demand an eye for an eye and a tooth for a tooth? Safe? Will you lie in your beds at night and strain at every sound, shudder at every movement in the darkness?" Barbour's voice whispered into silence. Then he held his arm rigid, his finger pointing at Loomis, and shouted, "But above all else, let us consider this, can a man violate the laws of nature with impunity? Can he take fire in his hand without burning? Can he spend his days and nights in dissipation and remain honorable? Can he violate the commandments of God and walk among those who hold these commandments sacred? Let him try," Barbour thundered, "and he will find in this life, that he has sown the wind and shall now reap the whirlwind. He has sown the wind among us. Let him reap the whirlwind in eternity!"

In total silence, the courtroom of people —
those on the jury, on the judges' bench, in the pub-
lic area — turned and regarded a pale and shaken
Loomis. Jumping to his feet, Loomis cried out in
protest, "But they were only Indians. Anyway, you
gonna listen to what a nigger says about what happened? I'm a *white* man. You best remember
that," he shouted at the jury. "I'm white, same as
you."

Judge Sweetz's gavel moved into action.
"Sheriff," he grated, "remove the prisoner to his
cell."

Hiram Winchell lifted Loomis from his seat as
easily as he might swing an infant in the air. When
order was restored in the courtroom, Sweetz advised the jury at length regarding the law. There
was, he said, summing up, no distinction in the law
as to nationality or color.

"The murder of an Indian is as criminal in law as
the murder of a white man. It is your solemn duty
to determine if the act of murder took place, and if
so, whether the defendant did willfully commit this
act."

The jury rose and shuffled on moccasin-clad feet
to the next room to consider their verdict. They
wrangled and swore at each other all during the
long night, but by morning they were agreed.

When court reconvened, the foreman stood and delivered the verdict: "Guilty of murder in the first degree."

Stopping leaped to his feet as soon as the foreman finished speaking. "I move for a new trial," he shouted.

Judge Sweetz said briefly, "Motion denied. The prisoner will stand and hear sentence passed." Loomis rose lazily to an upright position. "In my many years on the bench," Sweetz began, "never have I been confronted with so atrocious a crime, so unregenerate a criminal, so unspeakable a wrong committed against such innocent victims. We have come to this wilderness to build homes for ourselves and our families, to create a new state in a growing nation. As civilized human beings and good Christian people, we have a duty to this land and to its inhabitants. We have had to endure much. Have the Indians had to endure less?" He stared down at Loomis, slouching indifferently before him, and his voice began to shake with rage. "Why could you not have permitted these people to hunt and fish peacefully in their native forests? How could you have had the heart to war upon, shoot, and destroy women and children? Their blood goes up to heaven crying aloud for vengeance. Their blood rests upon all our consciences. It has imprinted a stain too deep to be washed out but by the blood of a Redeemer." The judge looked around the courtroom and then back at Loomis. "The sentence of this court is that you be hanged by the neck until you are dead."

9

——

AUGUST HAD ENVELOPED THE LAND in a suffocating embrace of sweltering humidity; September came in a rage of imprisoning rain, tearing across the terrain in torrential outbursts, pandemoniac winds lacerating trees and splintering bushes. The White River overran its banks; behind Jesse's cabin the gentle, placid creek became a swollen swift current of turbulent water. When the rain ceased at last, the land huddled forlorn and vanquished.

"The fence is down in two places," Chilili told her father gravely. "Maskanako will get through if they are not fixed."

Jesse smiled down at his sweet-faced daughter. "I'll take care of it right away."

Mekinges looked up from the kettle hanging in the fireplace in which she was stirring blue dye.

"You cannot keep Maskanako behind fences forever," she reminded Chilili. "The time will come when he must be set free."

"Not yet," Chilili cried rebelliously. "Not yet."

Takawsu burst into the cabin, followed by Sakkaape. "Tell him," Takawsu urged.

"Bad news," Jesse guessed, eyeing Sakkaape's sober expression. Sakkaape nodded grimly.

"Noble Loomis escaped. Pride Finch and Isaac Hamaker are coming. They want you to help them find Loomis."

"How did it happen?" Jesse asked.

Sakkaape quickly related what had passed. Loomis' son Tom and the two white men who had helped rob the Indians at the campsite had had individual trials, and all had been found guilty of murder in the first degree. All were in jail awaiting death by hanging. Fletcher Cornell and Simon Harmar, two of the men on the jury who had found Loomis guilty, had been drinking in Moses Wick's tavern. Yes, they admitted, they had gone along with the verdict, Loomis hadn't ought to have done what he did, but second thoughts were creeping in. Actually, when you got right down to it, wouldn't those Indians have done the same thing if they'd had a chance? Cornell and Harmar had killed a

119

few Indians in their time, Harmar muttered hoarsely, and he never felt they were worth the powder and lead it took to pick them off. And now Loomis and his boy Tom were going to hang. It wasn't as if they were horse thieves, Cornell sobbed in maudlin grief, or anything serious like that. And Loomis was right, white was white. No white man had ever been convicted in Indiana before, and by God no white man had ever been hung for an Indian before either. Somebody ought to go out to that jail and turn poor old Loomis loose, that's what somebody ought to . . . Cornell and Harmar turned bleary eyes upon one another, both struck with the same idea simultaneously. Weaving to their feet, the two men had staggered their way to the jail and managed to free Loomis, who had promptly fled in the direction of Jesse's house, vowing vengeance against Jesse before he shook the soil of Indiana free from his feet forever. The sheriff had been summoned by Isaac Hamaker, who had happened to glimpse Loomis and had learned from the now befuddled men who had released him about Loomis' threat. They had roused Pride Finch and Sakkaape, who had been a guest in Finch's house while he waited for his horse to be shod the next day. Sakkaape had ridden ahead to warn Jesse, but the others would be along soon.

Jesse had been examining his rifle carefully during the recital, and now said briefly, "All right, Sak-kaape. Let's go."

"The fence," Chilili cried. "You promised to fix the fence."

"Not now," Jesse said impatiently. "The fence can wait."

"But Maskanako will get out," Chilili pleaded.

"Not now," Jesse repeated brusquely and was gone. Chilili stared after him in hurt surprise. Never had Jesse refused her; she turned and looked at her mother with wounded eyes.

"He will fix the fence as soon as they have found the prisoner." Mekinges tried to comfort her daughter, but Chilili ran angrily from the room.

"Look to your sister." Mekinges caught Takaw-su's arm as he, too, turned to leave the cabin. Takawsu stared at her in surprise; he, Takawsu, when there was man's work to be done, to trail like a nursemaid to a girl?

"I must hurry to catch up with the others," he reminded his mother impatiently.

"Look to your sister," Mekinges repeated in a troubled voice. Takawsu's keen ear caught the plea behind the brusque command; nodding, he moved out of the cabin at a run, puzzling as to what harm Mekinges felt could befall Chilili. Did she think that Loomis was in hiding close by, and while the others were tracking him elsewhere, he would

121

strike, as he had threatened, at Jesse through the much-loved daughter? Takawsu considered the possibility and concluded that Mekinges' uneasiness was logical. Swiftly he followed his sister to the pen.

"Maskanako! Maskanako!" Chilili screamed. The wind tore the words from her lips. "He is gone. He has run down to the creek. The current is swift. He will drown," she shouted at her brother.

Chilili raced down the hillside, Takawsu close behind her. Now Ahtu, who had followed Jesse a short way when he had left the cabin and returned, joined Chilili, fur ruffling, ears pinned back by the gale.

"Maskanako will not go into the water." Takawsu tried to make himself heard above the roaring of the wind. He could see the young deer racing along the banks of the creek, joyful in its release, the call of the forest and its own kind stronger, more potent, than the sound of Chilili's beloved voice, windswept and forlorn. Takawsu caught Chilili by the arm. "Maskanako wishes to be free."

"No!" Chilili struggled away from her brother but even as she did so, her eyes beheld the bank give way and she saw the deer hurled into the swirling angry stream. "Maskanako! Maskanako!" She turned tear-brilliant eyes up at her brother. "He will die. He cannot stand on three legs in the leaping waters. He will die."

"He will not die," Takawsu said positively. "Deer can swim. Maskanako will swim until he can reach some safe place along the banks further down."

"Then I will follow," Chilili answered, setting her mouth in determined lines. "I will follow until I can find him and bring him back."

Slowly the two young people made their way along the path skirting the creek, leaping across trees lying broken in the wake of the storm across the trail, skirting battered branches, shivering as the relentless wind hammered away at their bodies. While Chilili had but one thought in mind — to rescue the three-legged deer — Takawsu wondered how the manhunt fared, whether Jesse and the others had picked up Loomis' trail, if Loomis was armed. As if in answer to this unspoken question, the sound of a shot split the air. Chilili froze where she stood, her body tense with shock.

"Maskanako!" she whispered.

Takawsu shook his head impatiently. "It is not deer they hunt, little sister," he reminded her. He, too, stopped to listen, but no further shooting came to their ears. He looked at his sister, who had once again begun to run along the banks of the stream. "Chilili," he called, but she did not turn. "Chilili!" He ran swiftly and when he reached her spun her about. "Chilili! You cannot follow Maskanako the length of the water. Go back. I will continue the search."

"No." Chilili pushed her brother aside and ran on. Ahtu looked from one to the other, then bounded to Chilili's side.

"Then go!" Takawsu shouted after her in exasperation. Was he to tag along after a small girl and a wayward animal when there was a man's work to be done? Was he a nursemaid, or a hunter? Defiantly, Takawsu turned back the way they had come. "I am not a nursemaid," he stopped to shout once, although his sister was long gone from view. "I am a hunter." At first he moved swiftly along the trail, but then a sense of uneasiness began to prevail, so that his steps slowed and finally stopped. Shrugging his shoulders, he turned and retraced his steps.

Chilili knew nothing of her brother's decisions; she had not even bothered to turn her head to see if he followed still, but had clung to one fixed idea — Maskanako, the three-legged one, needed her. She would rescue him from the cold turbulent waters.

"Maskanako," she called again joyfully. She had caught up with him at last, as he struggled to regain his foothold in the treacherous stream. The animal heard her voice and turned his head; his beautiful brown eyes momentarily quickened with hope. But Maskanako was not the only one whose heart quickened at sight of the small girl. Loomis, lying hidden in a hollow log, recognized the call; downcreek Stone Eater stiffened to attention. Loomis crawled stealthily from his hiding place. Jesse Benton's half-breed girl. This little half-breed would be his guarantee of safety, yes sir! Loomis ran a grimy hand, fingers stretched taut, back and forth under his chin. He began to inch his way out of the log but froze when he saw Ahtu turn her head sharply in his direction. That accursed wolf, he swore. Who but an Indian would keep a wolf as a pet? Rage spread through his body like the taste of bile in his throat. Were things never to go right for him? But now Ahtu's attention was engaged elsewhere; Stone Eater was moving stealthily toward the girl. Ahtu's large head swiveled from one to the other; she was puzzled; every fiber of her being recognized danger, but danger encircled. She did not know which presented the greater evil. At last she started toward Stone Eater, whose presence was more immediately apparent to her. At that moment the struggling deer found purchase on the bottom of the creek and rose to his feet. Loomis slithered from the log, his fingers digging into Chilili's shoulder even as she, having seen Maskanako coming toward her and the safety of the bank, uttered a triumphant cry of happiness. "Gotcha!" he bellowed, and, turning, caught a glimpse of Stone Eater's hate-ravaged face and the glint of sun on the Indian's poised rifle; swiftly, as Stone Eater's intent became clear, Loomis held Chilili in front of him as a shield. Even as the child fell at his feet, Loomis was speeding away, seeking safety in the woods. At the moment the rifle crackled, Ahtu flung herself with a howl of fury at Stone Eater, locking him in a prison of gnashing teeth and razor-edged, slashing claws.

Takawsu, meanwhile, having heard the shot, tore back along the path, his heart pounding. "Someone has shot Maskanako," he thought, but knew, when he saw his sister limp on the bank, the blue eyes lifeless, the spirit fled from her small body, that this nameless terror had hung over him since they had left the cabin. He kneeled beside Chilili and bowed his head.

"Little sister," he said brokenly. "Why could you not have listened to me? See? Here stands Maskanako. Did I not tell you he would not drown? Did I not say that no harm would come to him? Maskanako you named him, remember? 'He is strong,' you said. Maskanako. It is a good name." Takawsu looked up at the gentle deer,

whose deep brown eyes studied the little girl without comprehension. Takawsu rose to his feet. Ahtu, having finished her vengeful attack, came slowly to his side. Stone Eater had not died easily. Ahtu would bear the marks of his knife all the years of her life.

"We must take her home, Ahtu," Takawsu said. Tenderly, he lifted his sister and cradled her in his arms. Slowly he began to move back along the path, the burden in his arms lighter than the unbearable, tearing pain that consumed him. Obediently Ahtu followed, but Maskanako pawed the ground restlessly. Instinct called him strongly back to the forest; he took a few abortive steps away, then, tugged in the other direction by the bond of Chilili's love, trotted behind Takawsu. The wounded wolf, the tremulous three-legged deer, and the shattered boy were bringing Chilili home.

10

———

THE SOUND OF THE FALLING TREE reverberated through the forest. Jesse regarded it, tight-lipped and silent, then motioned to Takawsu to come close. Together, no word passing between father and son, they began to hack away at the fallen oak, chopping off a length of log, five feet of which they split off for boards. Father and son bent to the task grimly — the *che-pe-em-kuk*, the rough wooden coffin in which Chilili would lie, must be made ready for the funeral to take place the next day. Grief and guilt united and separated them. "Why didn't you stay with your sister?" Jesse had cried in anguish. "Why did you not fix the fence when she begged it?" Takawsu flashed back in anger. Mek-

129

inges had withdrawn from both. She hugged her sorrow and pain in some dark recess of her being, going about her household tasks as if nothing had disrupted them, a determined clinging to the norm which managed, nonetheless, to exclude both husband and son with finality. She had spoken only once to Jesse, to say mildly, as if the matter had little importance, that Chilili was to be buried in the cemetery of the Lenni Lenape, the burial ground which bordered the Wapahani. Jesse had opened his mouth to protest, had seen the look in Mekinges' eyes, and had nodded agreement; the only stipulation he made, adopting the same mild tone, was that Chilili would be laid in a coffin, and not lie above ground, as was the Delaware custom. Mekinges had agreed.

When the rude coffin was finally finished, Jesse and Takawsu walked to the burial ground. Skoligiso and others had offered to dig the shallow grave, but Jesse would not permit it. Everything Chilili needed he must prepare with his own hands; Takawsu's presence he tolerated because even in the depth of his grief he realized that the boy could not be shut out; Takawsu, too, must help the "little sister." Together they dug into the ground, stopping to rest only when they had reached about two feet in depth. Jesse stood erect, then, running the back of his hand across his forehead to remove perspiration from his brow. September, which had roared across the land like a rapacious marauder bent on destruction, now brought, as if in conciliation, the merest hint of a breeze, a gentle summer zephyr, clear flawless skies, and a palette of delicate color to the woods, a mosaic of yellows and greens and russets. Under the warming sun, the earth in this quadrangular field, a space consisting of some two hundred feet, took on a deep yellow tone. The burial ground was not enclosed, but here and there small rough fences made of saplings surrounded individual graves. Within these sapling-log fences, corpses rested upon the surface of the ground.

Takawsu stood apart from Jesse, his eyes following the slope of the land down toward the river, which moved placidly enough today, a ripple of sunlight lighting the water down to the bend. The eyes of father and son met briefly; wordlessly they bent once again to their digging. When at last they were done they went down to the river's edge and paddled back to the trading post. Mekinges noted their arrival incuriously; the day was beginning to deepen into dusk almost imperceptibly; it was time to prepare the evening meal. Jesse turned from the cabin and went to the pen where Maskanako nibbled haphazardly at the grass. Disregarding the deer, Jesse began to repair the fence. Takawsu followed his father to the pen. Now at last he spoke.

"Why do you fix the fence now?" he asked bitterly. Jesse did not raise his head. "I promised Chilili I would fix it. Later, I said. It is later now." The misery in his voice touched his son at last. Takawsu ran to his father and buried his face in Jesse's chest; Jesse caught him and held him tight. Mekinges, coming to call them, waited a moment at the crest of the hill, then turned stonily back to the cabin.

That night Mekinges went across the river to the village of her people, to lament with the women in the traditional manner. The sound of their mourning drifted faintly to Jesse's ears as he sat outside the trading post. The September night had an unusual clarity; the tops of the trees loomed dark against the moonlit sky; shadows painted the land softly. Takawsu stood and listened, then went into the cabin and up the ladder to the loft. He stretched out on the straw mattress, his arms folded under his head, and stared unseeingly at the roof. Tears stung his eyes, but he willed them not to fall. When sleep finally touched him, the tears escaped and coursed down his cheeks.

The next morning gleamed into brightness under a clear blue sky. When Jesse and Takawsu paddled across the river, they found that some of their friends had already assembled there — Pride Finch, Isaac Hamaker, Sakkaape — and stood silently waiting. It was not customary for a white man to participate in an Indian funeral, but this Indian girl was the daughter of a white man, therefore Jesse's friends were made welcome. The women had been busy before Jesse's arrival. Chilili's body lay upon a long board, secured to it by hickory withes whose ends dangled loosely from the board in six places. The little girl had been swathed in white muslin. At a sign from Mekinges, six women detached themselves from the onlookers. Silently each woman grasped the ends of the withes, three on each side of the bier. Now they lifted the board; Mekinges stepped in front of them. The funeral procession had begun. Mekinges led the way. After her came the six women, carrying the bier. Immediately behind them came the women of the village, all walking in single file. Jesse and the others had gone ahead to the cemetery; the men of the village had also assembled there, to build the fire that would free Chilili's spirit from her body.

The funeral cortege moved slowly, seeming to the men watching to appear and disappear in a grove of trees. At last they came to the gentle hill which sloped down to the burial ground. At the gravesite the women carefully placed their burden temporarily on the ground. While they waited patiently, Jesse and Takawsu took the boards they had split from the log the previous day and placed

them on the bottom and sides of the narrow opening in the grass-free soil. Now Hamaker and Finch loosened the withes; Sakkaape kneeled and lifted the little girl's body and placed it tenderly upon the boards. Stepping back, he watched somberly as Jesse covered the coffin with the remaining board, putting the lid across the nailless box with studied precision.

Mekinges stooped down and clutched a handful of dirt, letting it sift through her fingers onto the coffin. Her lips moved but she made no sound. Abruptly she turned away as one after another, first the women and then the men, repeated her action. Finch, too, scooped up a fistful of dirt. "Ashes to ashes," he said clearly as he relinquished the soil. "Dust to dust," Hamaker muttered in his turn. Jesse stood aside, his head slightly bowed. A prayer he had learned in childhood flashed into his mind. He spoke it aloud, painfully. *What is man that thou shoulds't care for him, or mortal man that thou shoulds't think of him? Man is like a passing breath, his days are like a flitting shadow.* He raised his eyes blindly. Smoke from the fire was being wafted by the caressing breeze into a spiral of mist reaching skyward; tinged with the merest suggestion of blue, it disappeared into the spreading green-leafed branches of the trees.

The silence in the cemetery was unbroken save

for the rhythmic sound of dirt against coffin; Sak-kaape was filling the grave. When the earth was high enough, he shaped it with care into a compact oblong mound.

Skoligiso raised a pole at the grave, from which a small white flag fluttered gaily in the breeze. The Great Spirit would have no trouble finding the little Chilili with the flag to guide him.

11

On the day of the hanging the crowds began forgathering at sunrise. The scaffold itself had been built north of the jail just at the rim of the bottom land. The dip in the valley placed the scaffold like a stage setting in the midst of the action to unfold; the surrounding low hills rose like tiers from the bottom land. As with a successful play, every seat for the spectacle was spoken for; the hillsides were dotted with spectators in holiday mood who had come long distances for this special occasion. The Lenni Lenape were present, too. Soon they would leave Indiana, as agreed with the United States government, which had purchased their land and would now move the Lenni Lenape

137

beyond the Masispek, the muddy water, called Mississippi, to the country known as Missouri. But this one last thing they wished to see — whether the punishment the white man had promised would happen. Miamis and Pottawatomis came also and sat apart from the others, silent and watchful. Laughter and chatter filled the air; the sun shone, a small breeze played with ribbons and skirts, hair, and feathers and teased the suspended nooses impartially, as it rustled leaves on branches overhead and hurried fallen leaves on the ground.

Suddenly, as if on signal, all sound ceased. Heads swiveled. Hiram Winchell was bringing the prisoners. The two accomplices appeared wild-eyed and trembling, the shock of the moment searing into their minds and bodies. Tom Loomis wore a vacant expression, as if reason had already fled; he stared about him uncomprehendingly, his jaw slack, spittle dribbling from a corner of his mouth. Only Loomis maintained his defiant attitude, glaring at the onlookers, greeting familiar faces with insolent asides. These people — hundreds of them, Loomis estimated — had come to see *him*, the star of the show, so to speak. Well, he'd give them something to see. He swaggered behind the others clear up to the scaffold. Momentarily he was staggered by the sight of four black coffins, neatly aligned in a row, thoughtfully positioned next to the scaffold; recovering, he turned and spat.

The silent crowd watched every movement, devoured every expression on the faces of the condemned men. Hamaker, Finch, and Jesse, looking on from the sheriff's office, wore grim, harried looks, like men for whom the distasteful battle had not yet been joined but lay inescapably ahead. Jesse Benton had been a bitter man the day he and Finch had recaptured Loomis, but neither he nor Finch had a taste for hangings. Jesse, eyeing Tom Loomis as the boy shuffled from the jail to the waiting noose, felt a stab of pity, for the boy had been led inevitably to this moment by the teachings of his father. Up on the hill, lost among the Lenni Lenape, Takawsu also fixed his glance upon Tom Loomis. Jesse had requested that Takawsu remain at home. Takawsu had not commented, nor had he acquiesced; when Jesse left, Takawsu quietly joined his people streaming to the hillsite. The sight of Tom Loomis, pathetic in his fear, his body trembling uncontrollably, stirred him not at all. Looking at Tom, Takawsu saw once again Tom's fingers digging into Chilili's arm, the knife held menacingly at Chilili's throat, the drops of blood spilling down her cheek, Chilili falling at Takawsu's feet. "You are dirt," Takawsu had said to Tom. "Now I wash your face in it. Another time I

139

will bury you in it." This day would see Tom buried. Takawsu's hatred was implacable; he was here to see Tom Loomis hanged.

Black masks were pulled down over the faces of the first two men to be hanged; their arms secured behind them, they were led to the nooses. At a signal from Winchell, the trap door beneath their feet was sprung; simultaneously, as the men fell, the crowd released a communal sigh.

The doctor came forth when the men were cut down. He pronounced them dead after a brief examination. Quickly the men were laid in their coffins. Noble Loomis now mounted the steps leading to the scaffold. He looked down and grinned at his son, sitting bleakly on his coffin, waiting his turn.

"Don't you fret none, Tom," he called. "We ain't dead yet."

The young man stared apathetically at his father. Noble had said it every day that had passed in jail; he had reiterated it when Hiram Winchell had come to fetch them to the hanging. He was clinging to this hope even as the black mask was being presented to him. A plea for clemency had been sent to the governor's mansion for Tom. A number of citizens had gotten together and signed a petition. The boy was so young, the petition argued; he had repented his part in the atrocity many times over; he had been led astray by evil companions. None of the townspeople had mentioned Noble's name, yet he had somehow persuaded himself that the governor would pardon Tom, and if Tom, certainly the father as well. Would it be fair, Noble had declaimed over and over, discussing the expected pardon with Tom in the cell, to stand by and watch a father hang? No one could expect it. It wasn't the human thing to do.

"And you sure know what the human thing is, don't you, Noble?" one of the other partners in crime had asked sardonically.

"If it wasn't for Noble in the first place, we wouldn't be in this jail," the other prisoner had said sullenly. Noble had turned on him fiercely and told him to keep his big mouth shut. "You were willing enough, it seems to me, when we jumped those Indians," he had shouted. "That wasn't my finger fired the shots from your rifle."

The three men had broken into acrimonious accusations; Tom had withdrawn to a corner of the cell and hunched down into it. He had witnessed death often, in many guises. He had gleefully participated, enjoyed the paralyzing fear that leaped into the eyes of victims, relished the pleas that begged for life, had discussed with gusto how each person had looked, taking as much pleasure from the rehashing of an incident as in the actual killings

141

themselves. But now death was different. It was happening to him, to *him*. He had never thought of death as something personal . . . someday, maybe, when he was an old man . . . but not now. It wasn't right; it wasn't fair. To visualize himself cold in his coffin, the sound of dirt falling on the lid — his mind withdrew from the horror as his body attempted to withdraw from the cell.

At first Tom had fastened to the hope that the governor would indeed pardon him. Like Pa said, it was the only human thing to do. It wasn't as if, he agreed with Pa, they had done any real harm. They hadn't touched anyone in the white community . . . it was Jesse Benton's fault, he had brooded when they were first thrown into jail. Making out like Indians were good as white people. Everybody knew they were just savages.

The black mask came down over Noble Loomis' face; his arms were tied behind his back; the noose was fitted carefully around his neck; the trap door was sprung. And then, as if in unison from one mass throat, a gasping sigh swept the crowd: just as the door opened and his feet brushed empty space, Loomis, in a last desperate attempt to stay death, broke loose from the confining cords that bound his arms and seized the noose that strangled him. He swung himself clear of the yawning void beneath onto the steady support of the wooden platform. With a triumphant gesture he tore the black mask from his face; his eyes glittering, his lips sneering, he shouted defiantly, "I ain't dead yet. The gallows ain't been built that can hang Noble Loomis. You hear that, Tom?" he called to his son, sitting and staring open-mouthed at his father.

Hiram Winchell stood, jaw agape, dumfounded at the scene he had just witnessed, then, recovering, he leaped forward to secure Loomis' arms again. But Loomis fought back savagely. Having jubilantly conquered death, he was determined to maintain his new lease on life. Hiram was a powerful man, and Loomis a weakling by comparison, but desperation gave him surpassing strength. The two men battled while all around the onlookers stayed aloof from the reality of the scene, spectators at a sport, moved as if to cheer gladiators in the arena. The Indians watched intently; some of the more superstitious among them regarded the incident as a portent. The white men began to call out indiscriminately, some giving obscene advice to the sheriff, others lending support to the embattled prisoner.

"You can't hang a man twice," Fletcher Cornell shouted suddenly. Up until Loomis' dramatic snatch at life, he had been observing the hanging with the detached air of a man who was whiling the time away as a matter of routine. Now, however, he felt suddenly called upon to have his moment in the sun. "He's all but died," Cornell went on. "I say he's paid the price. Let him go, Hiram."

Simon Harmar echoed Cornell's cry. "Yeh, let him go, Hiram."

A sharp-nosed woman nearby took up the cudgels. "Do your duty, Sheriff," she warned shrilly. "He's a murderer." She threw an oblique glance toward the silent Indians. "Honest folk don't want to be murdered in their beds because of him."

"Hannah's right," another woman yelled. "Hang the murderer!"

A feeling of restlessness seized the waiting crowd. Hiram, sensing that the hanging had better be expedited at once, shouted for his deputies, who, until now, had apparently been mesmerized by what was happening. Two men came to the scaffold on the run. Overpowered, the mask once again in place, his expression hidden from the viewers, and his arms held in a vise of cords, Loomis had scarcely time to understand that death was the master before he, like the two who had preceded him, was dangling limply at the end of the rope. So quickly had Hiram and his deputies sprung the trap door, the hanging was over before the crowd fully appreciated what it was they had witnessed. Loomis was cut down and placed in his coffin and Tom Loomis was being helped up the steps of the scaffold before the mass of people reacted. Now the mood had changed. They had come to see four men hanged; three men had danced with death before their eyes. But with the approach of Tom Loomis to the noose, vacant-eyed, trembling, a wave of sympathy rose up.

"He's suffered enough," the sharp-nosed woman muttered. "His own pa hanged right in front of him."

Others caught up the cry. "Let him go, Hiram. He's only a boy."

Tight-lipped and grim, Hiram Winchell pulled the black mask over Tom's face. The boy had been tried and condemned. It was not for Hiram Winchell to go against judge and jury.

Suddenly a new sound swept through the crowd. Arrested by the change in tone, Hiram paused before attaching the noose to Tom's neck. His eyes were caught by the sight of a horse and rider racing headlong in the distance, approaching the scene of the hanging at breakneck speed. Word traveled through the spectators more quickly than the galloping hoofs on the dusty road.

"It's the governor! It's the governor! He's come with the pardon."

Hiram waited. Now, his eyes narrowed to mere slits, he could make out the figure of the man on the horse. A smile hovered briefly about his lips. It

145

was the governor all right. No other horse in Indiana had trappings so richly decorative and pretentious; no other man would appear at a hanging dressed in a frock coat and high hat, or time his coming to the hairbreadth between life and death in so dramatic an action. Despite the size of the crowd, the air was so hushed the sound of the hoofs reverberated through the hills.

The governor held his head high and his face immobile. Arriving at last at the scaffold, he leaped lightly from the saddle and vaulted up the steps to snatch the mask from Tom's face.

"Do you know who I am?" the governor asked. His voice carried clearly, as the whisper of a trained actor reaches the upper balcony in a theater.

Tom tried to speak but could not. He shook his head. The governor swallowed his anger. "I will tell you who I am," he said in ringing tones. He turned and addressed the crowd. "In all this world, only two powers in the Universe can save this miserable wretch from the fate that awaits him. One is the Lord God Jehovah and the other is Governor James Brown Ray of Indiana. I am Governor Ray and do pardon him."

A cheer, low in key at first, but rising in crescendo as Hiram Winchell removed the cords from Tom Loomis' wrists, broke about the governor's ears. Smiling, he leaped from the platform,

mounted his horse, and rode away as spectacularly as he had come. Tom stood on the scaffold and watched in a daze.

"You can go now, Tom," Hiram said. "Don't you understand? You're free."

Tom stared at Hiram blankly. "Where'll I go?" he asked in a hoarse whisper finally. "What'll I do?" Hiram shrugged and walked away. Tom turned and stared at the three coffins, so neatly lined in a row, waiting removal to the cemetery. He walked down and sank to his knees. "Pa," he shouted, and began to pound his father's coffin, "where'll I go? What'll I do?"

In the sheriff's office, Jesse moved away from the window. He exchanged looks with Hamaker and Finch, both of whom shrugged their shoulders and raised their brows. Up on the hill, Takawsu's expression was black with hate. Abruptly he ran from the site, his eyes blind with rage, his feet guiding him instinctively home. Just as instinctively, when he at last reached the trading post, he moved beyond it to the pen, where Maskanako grazed tranquilly. The deer lifted his head, fixing his soft brown eyes upon the troubled boy. Then, as if in answer to some cry of need and anguish, he trotted to Takawsu and began, very gently, to nuzzle him.

12

OCTOBER – 1820
The Year Ends

THEY CAME QUIETLY down the Wapahani in canoes, from the adjacent countryside astride ponies, and from their village across the river to gather at Jesse Benton's cabin. The year had come full circle; once again it was the month of the broken moon, of the shedding of the leaves — Pōōkseet Kēēshooh, in the English calendar, October. The saddened remnant of a once powerful nation was leaving, as agreed with the white father in Washington, D.C., to take up the weary trek to new lands beyond the Mississippi.

The Indian agent had arrived well in advance and a tent had been pitched for him in the shade of a huge oak tree. Outside the tent a fallen maple lay stretched like a long rough bench; it would serve as such for the spokesmen for the Indians.

"I'll need a table to write on," Colonel Barron had said fussily, and when it was fetched he adjusted it minutely. The table proving too rough for the colonel, an aide had once again been dispatched to get a blanket to cover it. The aide was busily smoothing the blanket when Jesse Benton stepped out the cabin door and approached.

"You'll have to change the blanket, Colonel," Jesse said pleasantly. The colonel turned and stared, not taking kindly to any suggestions that did not originate with himself.

"I see nothing wrong with this blanket," the colonel replied coldly.

"It's red," Jesse pointed out, still maintaining his pleasant tone. "Red is the color of blood. It is a bad omen to the Delawares."

"Begging your pardon, sir," the aide broke in diffidently, "it's the only color blanket we have."

"Then they will just have to put their superstitions aside for today, won't they?" Colonel Barron gave Benton a small dismissing nod of the head, but Jesse stood his ground.

"If you want this removal to go smoothly," he insisted, "change the blanket."

The colonel opened his mouth to form a withering reply, but once again the aide interrupted.

150

"Colonel, look," he muttered. The colonel spun on his heels. With narrowed eyes, he took in the quiet approach on the river, the silent, mutinous air of those arriving on ponies. Suddenly his small group of soldiers seemed lost in an inundation of red men.

"Change the blanket," he barked at his aide.

"You can get a white blanket in the cabin," Jesse suggested. The aide broke into a run.

Jesse, watching, saw the aide reappear and Mekinges standing briefly in the doorway. His eyes clouded with anger and pain; she had not changed her mind, then, for she was dressed, ready to leave when the others did. He had argued; he had cajoled; he had threatened. Mekinges had remained adamant.

"You are a son, a brother, a husband of the Lenni Lenape," she had countered instead. "Why can you not go with the people to the far land beyond the Masispek?" she had asked quietly. "Do you not know they would welcome you among them?"

Jesse had stepped to the doorway and looked out. "I can't," he had answered at last, despairingly. "This land is too deeply bred in my bones."

"Perhaps so," Mekinges had agreed. Then she had added, in mingled anger and hurt, "And per-

151

haps it is also that you do not wish to spend the rest of your days with the Lenni Lenape. Once you were content to be hunter, trader, woodsman. Now more and more white people come. They build, and they make big plans. And they look to you to lead them. They have even given a village your name. The white people tie you to them with strong chains."

"They are my friends, Mekinges . . ."

"Once we were your friends, too!" she had cried bitterly.

Jesse had gone to Mekinges and placed his hands gently on her shoulders, pulling her close. "Life is changing, Mekinges. We can't stop it. And a man changes, too, with the times. But what we feel for each other has not changed," he had said urgently. "We can still have a good life together, you and I and Takawsu."

Mekinges had removed herself from the circle of her husband's arms. "When my people go, I will go with them," she had stated flatly.

"Why?" Jesse had demanded. "I got special dispensation for you and the boy. You don't have to leave. After all, this is your home," he had added, irritation and resentment beginning to tinge his voice.

Mekinges had turned then to look at him. "This has always been my home. It has always been the home of my people. We were content here, until your people came."

"My people?" Jesse had repeated, shocked. "*My people?*"

Mekinges had shrugged. "You are white," she had said, and turned away.

Frustrated, Jesse had flung himself out the door. Never had this arisen between them before. In truth, neither had even considered it. Jesse, having been born and raised, admittedly, by white people in an Indian village, speaking their tongue as fluently as they did themselves, knowing their customs . . . Momentarily his mind was diverted from the litany he recited mentally to earlier days, when he had moved in and out of the Delaware camps easily and naturally, and to a trick he had played on Skoligiso. He had dressed himself as a Shawnee, painting himself in the Shawnee manner, and had unobtrusively approached the Indian camp. At the periphery of the camp, he had seated himself upon a log, and had begun puffing away contentedly upon his pipe. Almost an hour had passed; oblique glances had been sent his way, but no one had approached. Then at last Skoligiso, in full dress, had walked slowly but purposefully to where the pseudo-Shawnee lounged. As Skoligiso had neared the log, Jesse had risen politely. The two had exchanged pipes, although neither one had uttered a word, and together, still silent, they had strolled back to the lodge. Inside the lodge, Skoligiso had indicated with a sharp gesture that Jesse was to seat himself upon a bearskin. This Jesse had done, careful to place himself with his back toward the consulting chiefs. But one of the chiefs studied Jesse constantly. At length he had risen from the council and shouted with great good humor, "You, Jesse Benton! You great Shawnee Indian! Welcome!" A gust of laughter had swept the lodge. Skoligiso, who could no longer keep a straight face, had bellowed, "You, Jesse Benton. Shawnee brave! You great representative of Tecumseh."

Remembering, Jesse smiled. Takawsu, coming upon him unexpectedly down the path and noting the smile, misunderstanding its meaning, turned away coldly.

"Wait," Jesse called urgently, but at that moment the aide came and summoned him to the council. Skoligiso and the others had arrived and were now seated upon the fallen log, waiting for Jesse to come and interpret the words of the Indian agent. Jesse was tempted to shake off the aide, to say angrily that the Lenni Lenape understood English well enough, that it was his son who was important at this moment, but he could not abandon his responsibility now, not to the tribe nor to the government for whom he had been appointed interpreter and spokesman. Suppressing a sigh, he turned and followed the aide to the site of the council.

Colonel Barron began speaking the moment Jesse reached the fallen log. "The great father in Washington, D.C., who has only your interest at heart," he began crisply, "has prepared a home for you beyond the Mississippi River. There you will grow as a nation. You will have new vigor, new strength." He waited, obviously impatient, while Jesse translated his words. The Indians sat listening without expression as first one and then the other man spoke. "You are no longer happy here," Colonel Barron resumed, "but in the new lands, your happiness will return, under the care of the United States government. The great father in Washington, D.C., will give you rations free of expense for one year after your arrival . . ."

When the colonel's speech at long last came to an end, Skoligiso arose, his stance dignified, his manner assured. His long black hair, tinged with gray, hung to his shoulders. For this occasion he had worn a jacket fashioned from a white quilt; around his waist he had tied a brilliant red sash.

"The colonel tells us our happiness will return. We look around and we say, our happiness fled when the white man came and took our land away. We were happy then . . ."

The colonel interjected quickly and angrily, "We did not *take* the land, Skoligiso. The white father paid for it."

"And did he pay for the air we breathe, the clouds above our heads, the sun in the sky, the rain that falls from the heavens?" Skoligiso cried. "We know that we must leave," he said heavily. "We are like persons traveling with packs on our backs, not knowing where the path will lead us. The land on which we expected to live out our lives has been sold from us. But we will not wait now for the money to be paid to us when we cross the Masispek, the muddy water. Let the white father pay us now. Let Jesse Benton pay us for the white father this day, before we go."

Colonel Barron fumed, but the Lenni Lenape were adamant. Their annuities had been paid to them last year, and they wished Jesse to pay the annuities again. Word spread through the groups of Indians waiting for the council to end, to those seated engaged in earnest conversation beneath a huge oak, those who were eating in their wigwams, the men who were gambling, running races, and the younger braves playing *yah-yout-tche-chick*, the game of skill which was like the game the white men played with horseshoes, pitching them at a fixed peg over an established distance. The women and children, too, were summoned. All began to form small family groups on the field between the trading post and the Wapahani. Takawsu came, and Sakkaape, to distribute sticks among the people. To the older men, Takawsu and Sakkaape gave the longest sticks; to the next group in age they gave somewhat shorter sticks; the youngest men received the shortest sticks. Clutching their sticks, the Indians stood gravely waiting for Jesse. With Takawsu and Sakkaape at his side, Jesse now walked among the Lenni Lenape for the last time. The amount of silver dollars Jesse handed to each man depended upon the length as well as the number of sticks each one held. In exchange, the Indian relinquished the sticks he gripped to either Takawsu or Sakkaape.

No one left the prairie until each stick had been exchanged for money. When it was done, Skoligiso returned to the council.

"Satisfied?" Colonel Barron barked. Skoligiso nodded. He waved his hand at the families still assembled in the field; immediately they began to disperse, each Indian moving to return to what had occupied him before the distribution of the annuities.

Skoligiso resumed his seat upon the fallen log. Barron fussed with papers spread before him on the white blanket. Jesse stood halfway between the table and the log, lost in thought.

I stand equally distant from both, he brooded dismally. I do not take my place among the white men, nor do I stand with the red men. Once I did not question where I stood. I knew only the land, and my love for it, and the people, and I was content. Lifting his head, he caught a glimpse of Takawsu and Sakkaape joining Mekinges at the trading post. He compressed his lips, as if to keep his bitterness contained. Nothing he had said could convince Mekinges to stay. When Chilili had died, she had turned away from him forever.

"You did not fix the fence," she had cried. "She is dead because you did not fix the fence."

"Don't you think I tell myself that a hundred times a day?" Jesse had flashed back, anger compounded by guilt. "But how was I to know? *How was I to know?*"

Mekinges had remained silent. Reason had told her that she was flagellating him without cause, but emotion overrode reason. Chilili had pleaded; Jesse had ignored the plea and gone off in search of the white man. Now Chilili lay across the river, the beautiful deep blue eyes closed, the warm, compassionate heart stilled, her spirit called from her body by Manito.

"Mekinges," Jesse had said, speaking quietly. "If you go now, everything I have loved will be gone. Do not take the boy. I beg of you. Do not take Takawsu."

Mekinges had shrugged. "It is the way of my people," she had replied. "The young stay with the mother."

"He is not a child any longer. He is a young man."

"He is of the Lenni Lenape." She had regarded Jesse with blazing eyes. "Do you think I have not heard how your people speak of him — 'Jesse's half-breed kid,' " she had quoted savagely. "When we go beyond the muddy water, we shall have land of our own again, this the white father in Washington has promised. And Takawsu shall be a brave, and sit in the councils of his people."

Jesse had hunched his shoulders and moved to the doorway. "Ask him," Mekinges had called after him triumphantly. "Ask Takawsu. See which one of us he chooses." Jesse had not replied. He had seen Mekinges' sorrow and bitterness reflected in his son's eyes. Takawsu carried his own heavy burden of guilt; he would not choose to stay, with Chilili's fresh grave to remind him of the little sister whom he had cherished.

Jesse brought his thoughts back to the present, suddenly aware that someone was speaking to him,

160

had been trying to catch his attention for some time.

"Benton! Are you ill, man?"

Jesse stared at the colonel, bristling with irritation at being ignored. "What?" he asked in confusion.

"I said, now that all the details have been dispensed with," the colonel roared, "can we get them started?"

Skoligiso stood up, as did the other members of the council. He moved to Jesse's side. "We shall not forget you, Jesse Benton."

Jesse answered soberly, "Nor I you, Skoligiso."

The signal was given. The chief took his place at the head of the procession. Some, the elderly, the ailing, rode in wagons. Many walked. Still others sat astride ponies. Mekinges, Takawsu at her side, sat on a pony. Behind her was a string of sixty ponies, Jesse's farewell gift. She had not demurred; ponies would be needed. The procession, accompanied on either side by soldiers, began to move. Suddenly Jesse felt a hand on his shoulder.

"Sakkaape," he said in surprise, noting Sakkaape's horse, the saddlebags full, all his equipment packed.

"You have been my good friend," Sakkaape said quietly. "I shall remember you all the days of my life. But I am going with them."

"Why?" Jesse asked. "Why?"

"Because there is no place for me here. White people keep coming. There is a village now, where once there was only wilderness. Soon there will be cities, like there are in the East. Here I will never be more than a slave who's been set free, but to some and their way of thinking, still a slave. Out there" — Sakkaape's arm swept the air in a wide arc — "I'll be just another man, black, somewhat different, maybe, but a man. You understand how I feel?"

Jesse nodded. "I understand," he said. "But I wish to God I didn't," he added bitterly.

Sakkaape swung up on his horse. Almost as an afterthought, he removed the silver chain and disk from around his neck. "I won't be needing this anymore. I'd like you to have it."

Jesse took the chain and disk wordlessly. Then he nodded again. As Sakkaape began to ride off to join the procession, Jesse called after him, "Look after them." Sakkaape turned in the saddle and waved his hand in reply.

Jesse stood and watched the procession move by. Mekinges did not look back, but Takawsu, just before the dip in the hill hid him from view, turned and held his hand high in a gesture of farewell. Jesse followed them with his eyes until soldiers and Indians had all disappeared from his sight, waiting until the dust in the road, kicked up by the horses and ponies and wagons as they rumbled down the trail, ceased swirling in the cool October breeze. Then he walked slowly to the pen, where Maskanako nibbled grass daintily, and opened the gate. Maskanako lifted his head, then, as if puzzled, approached Jesse in the opening, his eyes seemingly inquiring. At last Maskanako stood in the opening, tossing his head from side to side, waiting for some word from Jesse. Jesse ran his hand gently over the deer's flank, then gave him a light slap on the rump.

"There's nothing to stay here for anymore," Jesse said. "Go ahead," he urged, "before I change my mind."

Maskanako moved through the gate, slowly at first, and then feeling his freedom, headed for the forest in a gamboling trot. He turned once, to look back briefly, then broke into a run.

Jesse stood and looked about him, at the gentle hills, the looming forest behind the cabin, the prairie sweeping down to the river. Overhead, hidden in the russet and yellow foliage, a cardinal scolded, *chuh, chuh, chuh, chuh*; a squirrel appeared, sat, and stared at Jesse, its bushy tail alert, its eyes bright and unwinking, then fled up a tree trunk and disappeared. Behind him, Jesse could hear the forest sounds, the skitterings and rustlings in the underbrush and trees, the creek purling its way through the woods, all the woodnotes that had filled his days. But the sounds he longed most to hear he would never hear again — Chilili speaking earnestly to a tiny creature barely clinging to life, Mekinges moving quietly about in the trading post, Takawsu hunting, fishing, working at his side, Sakkaape's deep voice, the Lenni Lenape's soft speech.

Jesse moved away from the pen, the gate still gaping wide, and walked with a slow step back to the cabin. Then he entered and with careful precision, as if it mattered greatly, he turned and closed the door.